ZEALOTS AND ZENITHS

Other books in the

Weary Dragon Inn Series

Ale and Amnesia *(Newsletter Exclusive)*

Drinks and Sinkholes

Fiends and Festivals

Secrets and Snowflakes

Beasts and Baking

Magic and Molemen

Veils and Villains

Zealots and Zeniths

Campaigns and Curses

Perils and Potions

Royals and Ruses

ZEALOTS AND ZENITHS

Weary Dragon Inn
BOOK SEVEN

S. Usher Evans

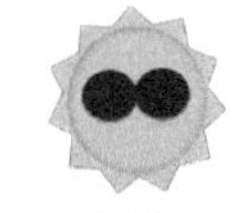
Sun's Golden Ray
Publishing

Pensacola, FL

Version Date: 6/22/24
© 2024 S. Usher Evans
ISBN: 978-1945438851

Map created by Luke Beaber of Stardust Book Services
Line Editing by Danielle Fine, By Definition Editing

Sun's Golden Ray Publishing
Pensacola, FL
www.sgr-pub.com

For ordering information, please visit
www.sgr-pub.com/orders

Dedication

To NHE

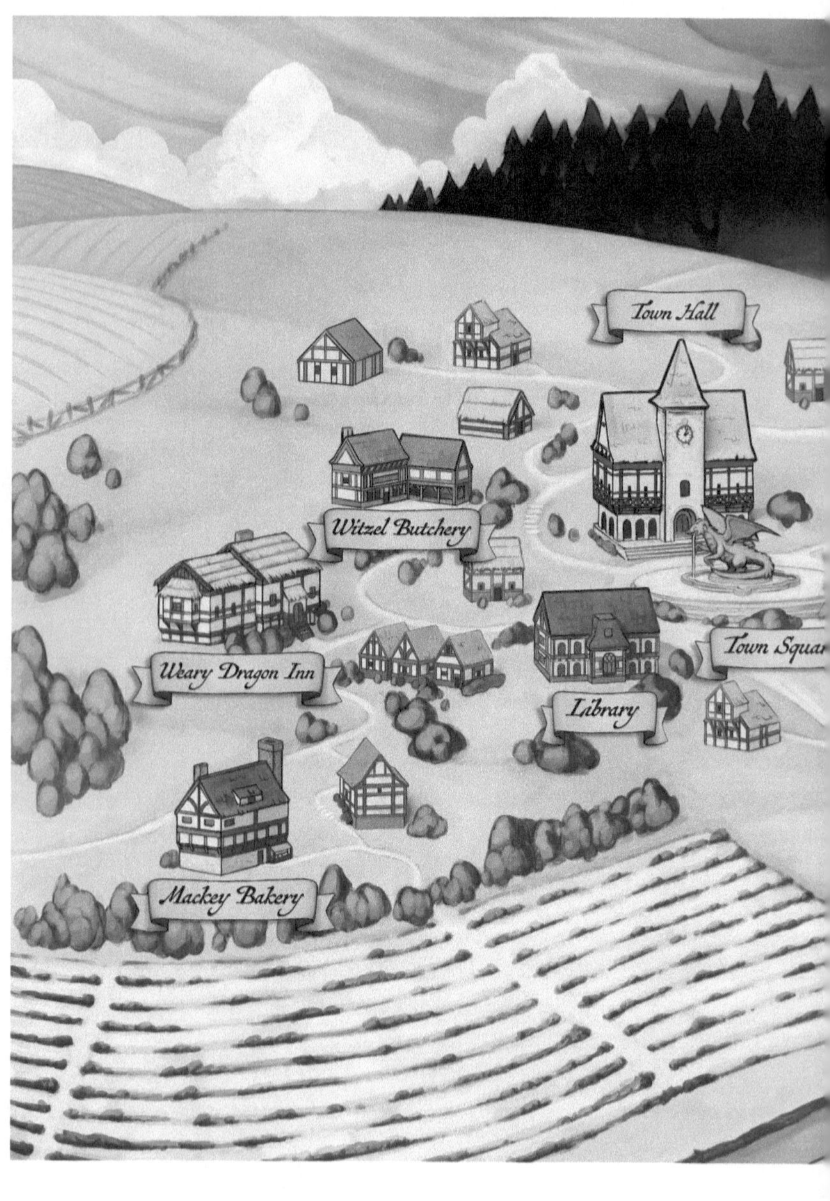

Town Hall
Witzel Butchery
Weary Dragon Inn
Town Squar
Library
Mackey Bakery

Pigsend Tea Shop
Flour Mill
Pigsend Village

Chapter One

"Leaving already?"

It was barely five in the morning, but the summer sun had already made its appearance. Which meant Bev's overnight guests at the Weary Dragon Inn were doing the same, ready to hit the road and make the most of the long day. Last night's guests included a trio of young merchants who'd requested separate rooms, a bard (who blessedly kept his lute to himself), a couple traveling to their son's wedding, and an old woman who was seeing the country before she was too infirm to do so. She was the last of Bev's guests to depart, and Bev had hoped the sweet dear might stay a little longer, at least so Allen the baker would have someone to appreciate his breakfast pastries.

"I wish I could, but I've got to take advantage of all this sunlight," the old woman said with a smile as she walked toward the door. "On my way to see what the Middleburg fuss is about!"

Then she was gone, and Bev had the unfortunate task of telling Allen that he'd baked muffins for nothing when he walked in ten minutes later.

"Suppose I've got to get over here earlier, don't I?" he said, his shoulders slumping as he put the full basket on the counter. "Maybe Biscuit wants one. Where is he, anyway?"

Bev thumbed toward the kitchen where her laelaps, a magic-detecting creature who resembled a small, golden-furred dog, was presumably sleeping.

"He was up all night, pacing my room," Bev said. "The strangest thing."

Allen frowned. "Is he sick?"

"I don't think so." Bev shook her head. "He's eating normally, smiles when I talk to him, wags his tail. But he gets in these moods where he scents something and can't stop sniffing for it. Sometimes it's hard to snap him out of it."

"Hm." Allen shook his head. "Maybe it's the solstice? Strange things happen sometimes, you know. Remember all that snow we had over the winter?"

Bev shrugged. "Maybe. Who knows with him, though, eh?" Bev helped herself to one of the muffins. "Maybe Etheldra will be able to sell them for you."

"Hope so," Allen said. "Speaking of, do you think I could ask her to pay me back for the wedding? Vicky says I should, but she's all the way in Sheepsburg, so it's easy for her to say."

Bev chuckled. Allen and Vicky Hamblin, the seamstress's apprentice, had been engaged and keen to put on the most extravagant wedding Pigsend had ever seen in order to impress Vicky's snooty aunt. But they'd encountered mishap after mishap, until it was revealed that Vicky's other aunt had cursed the wedding to gain access to Vicky's secret inheritance. But the curse had also uncovered the truth about Vicky and Allen—that perhaps marriage wasn't for them after all. Instead, Etheldra Daws, the taciturn tea shop owner, and Earl Dollman, the carpenter, had gotten married, and the wedding had been as beautiful and wonderful as any Bev had been to. Vicky had left with her snooty aunt to Sheepsburg to sort out the inheritance and perhaps see the world.

"I don't know if I'd want to broach that subject with Etheldra, but maybe Earl can when they get back from their honeymoon," Bev said. "So you've been writing to Vicky?"

"Oh, yes. We exchange letters about once a week." When Bev gave him a curious look, he waved his hand. "I still care for her very much. And she cares for me. But we agreed it's best that we go our separate ways for now. If fate has us rekindling things, we'll cross that bridge when we come to it."

Bev smiled. "That all sounds very mature."

"I'll tell you one thing: I never want to have anything to do with a wedding like that ever again," Allen said with a shake of his head.

Bev couldn't agree more. "I'm glad you two are staying in touch, though. I know Apolinary misses having her help at the seamstress shop."

"I told her I'd keep an eye on Grant, too," Allen said. "Apparently, he's decided he wants to be a farrier like PJ Norris, though I think it's just an excuse for the two of them to cut up. Valta Climber says she wants to be a farrier, too, but her parents told her no."

"I'm sure Grant's got his reasons for wanting to stick close to his friend." Number one being PJ was a dragon shifter, and Grant and Valta wanted to stay to make sure he didn't have any more episodes. But Allen, as beloved as he was, didn't know that. If anyone found out, especially a queen's soldier, the young boy would be arrested immediately and taken away.

Allen, who never really thought much of Grant, shook his head. "Would be nice if he'd help out at the bakery. We're up to our eyeballs in orders for the solstice."

"That's good, isn't it?" Bev asked. "Money in,

and all that."

"Yeah, we're just working like mad to get it all done," Allen said. "As much as that wedding was a nightmare, it really was great for my client base. People raved about Lillie's wedding cake, and she made a special pie for Kaiser Tuckey a few weeks ago. Suddenly, we're swamped."

"I'm glad you two are still working well together," Bev said. "And that she's been good for business. Lots of solstice pies, then? It's been a banner year for produce. I'm sure there's plenty at the market."

"I'd say we're buying up all the fruit as fast as it can grow, but no matter how many crates of peaches, berries, and plums we buy, there's always more the next day," Allen said.

Bev had seen the same when she'd visited the farmer's market the other day. "Maybe I'll have to buy one of those pies, then. Perhaps for the solstice. Might be nice to do something special for whoever's in town that day." She paused. "Or maybe I'll make one myself."

"Missing bread that much?" Allen said with a laugh.

Bev sighed. With the temperatures climbing, it was hard to time proofing her bread. One could fire up the oven to warm a place in the winter, but it was impossible to cool it down in the summer. Not to mention, having the oven on when things were already sweltering wasn't Bev's idea of fun. So Bev had, for the first time in months, *not* made her bread the night before.

"Etheldra's going to be furious when she gets back from her honeymoon," Bev said.

"She'll survive," Allen said with a laugh. "But it'll be cooler again in no time. Chin up, Bev!"

~

As much as she wished otherwise, cooler temperatures were far off. Summer was Bev's least favorite time of year. Not only because she could no longer make her award-winning bread, but it also heralded the anniversary of the day Bev had arrived in town. *Six* years since she'd awoken in Wim's garden, staring at the blue sky without a clue who she was or where she'd come from. Of course, now she had a few more clues, some certain, others an open question. And she was hoping that in the next few days, Vellora Witzel's old commander would arrive and put many of those questions to rest.

The butcher had been a soldier in the king's army, and had been in a particularly gruesome battle —one Bev seemed to have a memory of. Bev wasn't exactly sure it was *her* memory, because she only had it when she touched an amulet called a wizard's helper. It was entirely possible the bloody scene was the amulet's memory, not Bev's, and she was just the unfortunate person who'd managed to activate it.

Possible, but something in Bev's gut told her

that innocent view of things wasn't likely to be reality.

Vellora's commander had been high-ranking in the war, and Vellora thought he might know more about the powerful magical wielders who'd also been at the battle. So she'd written to him, and at Allen and Vicky's not-wedding a few weeks before, Vellora had told Bev the commander would be arriving today and staying through the solstice. Bev had been a bit on edge the past few days, wondering if he'd recognize her immediately or if this was all a big waste of time.

She pondered those questions as she left the kitchen to check the sheets she'd washed earlier. In the hot sun, they were already dry and ready to be put away for the next round of guests. Bev pulled them off the line, the sun burning the back of her neck as she worked, and tried to keep a positive attitude as she carried them back inside.

Just beyond the kitchen door, propped open to allow maximum airflow, Bev's trusty magic-detection creature, Biscuit, was pacing the floor again, his nose pressed to the ground. Bev placed the basket on her kitchen table, watching him for a few moments.

"You all right, Mr. Biscuit?" she asked, eyeing him.

He stopped, looked at her, and wagged his tail furiously, his tongue unfurling from his mouth as he smiled.

"You let me know if there's anything I can do," Bev said with a chuckle as she carried the laundry toward the stairs.

It took no time to fold, and after checking each of the empty rooms again to ensure they met her standards, she returned downstairs to continue her daily chores. Without the bread to contend with, there were fewer things on the list, and Bev missed the scent of yeast, flour, and rosemary. Lillie, the magical baker who lived next door, had offered to help out with the process, using her pobyd magic to infuse the dough so it wouldn't overproof, but Bev had declined. Bev's rosemary bread was her own version of magic, and to include someone else in the process felt wrong. Not only that, but one never knew when a queen's soldier might arrive, and they would be *very* interested in a full pobyd.

Bev tapped her fingers on the front desk where she usually greeted her guests for the night. It was morning still, and she doubted she'd see anyone until later in the afternoon. Longer days meant longer travel times, and it wasn't uncommon for her to get guests near nine o'clock these days. Another strike against the summer season.

Without anything else to do, Bev decided to pay her friends at the butcher shop a visit a few hours early and see if Andres had arrived yet. Across the street, Ida was hard at work dressing a pig, while

Vellora was working on a large cow. The smaller of the two, Ida, had supernatural strength and demonstrated it as she hoisted another perhaps three-hundred-pound pig onto the hook.

"Oh, morning, Bev!" Ida said as the bell above the door tinkled. "What's on the menu tonight?"

"Not sure," Bev said, sidling up to the counter and smiling at the two of them. "Just here for a social visit."

"Things that quiet at the inn?" Ida said with a laugh. "Shouldn't you be bustling?"

"I am, when it's dark," she said. "But the sun's up around five these days and doesn't go down until late." She made a face. "Ready for the summer to be over."

"It's a long time until then," Vellora said, wiping her brow. "Unfortunately."

"Oh, buck up, you two! At least there isn't snow up to your knees out there," Ida said. "And Bev, you should be happy things are quiet. Especially after all the excitement of Allen's…erm… Etheldra's wedding."

Ida was right about that. "Suppose it is nice that the only thing to talk about is dinner. Which, speaking of…" Bev smiled. "What do you have that's quick to cook?"

"What, don't want to slave over a hot oven all day?" Ida asked with a chuckle.

"Pork loin could be done quickly," Vellora said.

Bev eyed Vellora, finally deciding to ask the question she'd come here for. "Erm, when do you think your commander will arrive?"

"Hard to say," she said. "Later this evening, I'd guess. It's quite hot to be traveling during the midday hours."

Bev nodded, trying to keep the nerves off her face. "Well, better make sure I do something nice for him. Maybe I'll pop down to the market again and pick up some fruit. Allen says the farmers are overrun with it."

"It is that time of year," Ida said.

~

Bev's trusty mule Sin was getting up there in age, and the heat might make her ornerier, so Bev left her in the stable. Biscuit had finally stopped pacing and was fast asleep on the hearth, so Bev left him, too. She wasn't planning on getting a full slate of produce, just something to accompany dinner this evening. Peaches sounded lovely, so perhaps a compote with some sage from Bev's garden.

On the road ahead, a short man with a domed head and pronounced jaw pushed a large cart filled with produce. He wore a scowl, as if everything in the world offended him, which was truer than not. He didn't acknowledge Bev at all, so she decided to be the nice one and greet him first.

"Morning, Officer Nog," Bev said.

The man tripped over his feet and glared at her.

"Don't be *callin'* me that out here!"

"Nobody's around," Bev said, gesturing to the empty road. But point well taken. "How are things where you are?"

"Fine." He adjusted his grip on the cart. "Dandy."

He kept walking and Bev shook her head. The goblin (who was wearing a potion to make him look human) lived in a hamlet called Lower Pigsend, which held all the magical creatures the queen had outlawed. Bev's dear friend Merv, a six-foot moleman, had taken her there, and embroiled Bev in a search for a missing talisman. Long story short, Officer Nog was now on the hook for ferrying fresh produce from the farmers' market to the citizens down below as penance for his role in keeping the citizens in the dark. Bev saw him every time she visited the market herself, and he hadn't once seemed happy to see her.

Bev chuckled and continued on to the farmstands set up along the road. But when she approached, she could scarcely believe her eyes. She'd been here a few days ago, and the produce had been plentiful. But today, it was practically overflowing with every kind of fruit and vegetable she could imagine. It wasn't just the quantity, either. The onions were the size of a child's head; next to that were tomatoes so red and plump they looked on the verge of bursting. Blackberries and blueberries and strawberries and raspberries—fruit that should've been at the tail-end of its season—were as bright and perfectly ripe as they'd been earlier in the spring. Even the winter leafy greens were still vibrant.

"Morning, Bev!" farmer Alice Estrich said, waving her down. The other farmers watched Bev warily, perhaps hoping she might visit them, too. They certainly had enough fruit to get on with. "What can I sell you today? Clearly, I have a little bit of everything."

"Clearly," Bev said with a laugh. "I don't think I've ever seen so much produce in my life. What do you think's going on?"

"Haven't a clue." She shrugged. "I can't sell it fast enough. I pick the plants clean then, the next morning, I come out to find them full again." She gestured to the berries. "These won't go bad, either. Been waiting for them to get softer so I can make jam, but they don't want to. So I figured I'd sell 'em. Got plenty more at home anyway."

"Interesting," Bev said. "But I'll take some peaches. Got my mind on a compote this evening for some pork. Too hot to do anything too long in the oven."

"Can I interest you in some rhubarb, too? Maybe a strawberry-rhubarb solstice crumble could be on the menu?" Alice asked. When Bev declined, she wilted. "Drat. Bathilda threatened to run me off if I brought any more to her front door."

"Well, we can't have that." Bev chuckled. "How is Bathilda?"

"I'm a little worried about her." Alice sighed. "She's become something of a recluse lately. She'll barely open the door for me."

Bev hoped she wasn't involved in another round of mischief. The farmer had once kept an illegal herd of magical sheep on her property, but had told Bev the effort was more than the gold she'd received for them.

Alice lifted a peach and smiled. "Please take a bit more?"

"I think I can only carry one crate," Bev said, apologetically. "But if the weather's nicer tomorrow, I might pack up Sin and we'll get some goodies. I know the bakers have been making a ton of pies. Surely, they'll be by to get more from you."

She sighed, offering Bev a bunch of spinach, which should've been rotten by now. "Maybe a spinach salad? No charge. Just want to get it off my hands."

"Oh, all right." Bev put it on top of her peaches. "Thanks. Take it easy, Alice."

"I'll certainly try."

Chapter Two

Bev returned to the inn, humming to herself as she carried in the peaches and spinach. Instead of a salad, she'd wilt the spinach with some bacon and serve it up that way. She examined the leaves closer, looking for any sign of bruising or age. But they looked as freshly picked as ever, which seemed…odd for this time of year.

"Well, it is the solstice," Bev muttered to herself as she walked through the backyard of the inn toward the kitchen. But as her gaze landed on her garden, she stopped short, blinking.

When she'd done her chores earlier in the morning, her herbs had been a normal size. Leafy marjoram, vibrant parsley, and her rosemary bush, which she'd carefully propagated after it had come to an unfortunate end thanks to another magical-detection creature, had been robust, but managed.

Now, the vines and leaves spilled over the raised wooden bed, and the rosemary bush came to mid-thigh.

"Well, all right then," Bev said with a laugh. She would have to spend some time pruning her herbs and drying them out later—especially the rosemary, which would be in high demand once she was back to making bread.

She snipped some sage, though, and tossed it on top of the peach basket then continued into the kitchen. Biscuit popped up, his tongue unfurling as he welcomed her home with a tail wag.

"Feeling better?" Bev asked.

He jumped to his feet and trotted over, standing on his hind legs and sniffing the basket of peaches.

"You can have some peach skins after I'm done peeling them." She settled at the kitchen table with her paring knife and began to work, humming to herself. The skin slid off the juicy peaches with ease, and before long, Bev's fingers were covered in sticky syrup. As promised, she tossed a sliver of skin down to a waiting Biscuit, who gobbled it up in a single gulp.

"Only one," she said, grabbing the next one. "I'm already worried you might be sick."

He let out a whine.

"Oh, fine. As long as you're feeling all right."

Another piece of skin gone.

Alice had certainly given her a large number of peaches, more than she needed for a compote, but she added as many as she could to her stock pot along with a good heaping of sugar and some juice from a lemon. Once all that was combined, she finely chopped the sage and added that, letting the whole mixture simmer.

"Well, if this doesn't turn out, it would be delicious on some bread," Bev said to Biscuit, until she remembered she wasn't baking bread today. She did, however, have to maintain her dough by feeding it a little flour and water every day, even if she didn't bake with it. It was sitting on the counter in its usual place, and Bev could practically hear it crying forlornly at the thought of not being used.

"It's too hot," she said to no one in particular.

The compote was bubbling nicely, filling the kitchen with the warm scent of peaches and sage, when the front door opened. A pair of older gentlemen, one quite tall and thin, the other short and stout, walked in, each carrying a suitcase. Bev's first guests for the night.

The taller one, who introduced himself as Stephen Shepard when Bev came out to greet them, had bronze skin, sharp cheekbones, and spoke softly. The shorter one, Feliciano Mendel, was quite pale, with a ring of brown hair around his bald head.

"Just in town for the night, then?" Bev asked, scribbling their names down in her book.

"Erm." Stephen shared a look with Feliciano. "Perhaps."

"Would it be all right if we booked a few nights?" Feliciano asked.

"Of course," Bev said. "Don't have any reservations on the books at the moment. Will sharing a room be all right?"

It was, and the gentlemen thanked her for her hospitality and spoke eagerly about the dinner that was to come. Bev handed over their key and listened for the door to close before returning to the kitchen to check on the meal. But the fire in the oven was sweltering, so she and Biscuit sought refuge out in the main room again.

"Going to be a long season," Bev said to the laelaps.

~

Around five, as Bev was pulling the pork out of the oven, the second guest arrived, introducing themselves as Solan Brambilla. They had a long sheet of straight black hair that almost sparkled in the light and a striking pair of gray eyes. Biscuit's tail wagged as they drew closer, and Bev had to tsk at him to keep the laelaps from being too interested in the guest.

"One night?" Bev asked.

"Oh, no, no." Their voice had an airy quality,

and their attention wandered around the room. "Bad luck to travel on the solstice. I'll be here until the day after, at least. Depends on how the moon feels."

Bev cleared her throat. She *did* get all kinds here at the Weary Dragon. "Well, you'll be in room two. Dinner's at six."

"Lovely."

The unique individual picked up their suitcase, which was ratty and bulging with unknown contents, and swept up the stairs, humming to themselves.

"You leave them alone," Bev said to Biscuit, who'd trotted to the bottom of the stairs. "They're our guest, understand?"

The next person to arrive wanted a night, as they'd be leaving at first light to continue to Sheepsburg, and the next had a similar story, though they were headed south. Four of the six rooms were rented by the time Bev brought dinner out, which was quite normal for this time of year. She'd probably get a few stragglers as the sun set later in the evening, so she always kept a bit of dinner set aside in case they were hungry.

At six on the dot, Bev's usual cadre of folks arrived. Bardoff Boyd, the schoolteacher, greeted her warmly with a handshake, and Max Sterling, the librarian, was excited about the compote, but expressed sadness that there was no bread this evening.

"And I'm not the only one," Max said with a grimace.

At that moment, Etheldra Daws—who'd declined to change her name—and Earl Dollman walked in. Etheldra, an older woman with white hair and a sharp expression, certainly didn't have the glowing happiness of a newlywed, but her husband Earl did. Bev had never seen the carpenter looking so relaxed or joyful, as he slid his hat off and waved hello.

"Aren't you two a sight for sore eyes?" Bev said. "How was your trip?"

"Too long," Etheldra snapped.

"It was lovely," Earl said, used to Etheldra's bluntness. "Vellora told us to visit the southern shores, so we did. It was incredible. The sea was—"

"There was too much sand. Too many children. Everything cost twice what it should," Etheldra said, shaking her head with a scowl.

"Goodness me," Bev said. "Are you all right, Etheldra?"

"She's a bit tired from the trip," Earl said, placing a gentle hand on her shoulder. To her credit, Etheldra didn't shove it off, though she looked like she wanted to. "And things at the tea shop—"

"Absolutely outrageous what that Shasta Brewer did!" Etheldra bellowed, earning a curious look from the other diners in the room. "Everything was in the wrong place. Can you imagine putting mint tea next to the lavender? It's a wonder the shop didn't fall into ruin while we were gone." She stopped right where Bev usually had a basket of rosemary bread. "And *what* in the world is this? Where's my bread?"

"Too hot to make it, unfortunately," Bev said, having rehearsed this conversation a few times in her head in case the couple returned this evening. "The dough disintegrates. Even in the root cellar. I think I'll—"

"Then go next door and get that Lillie girl to fix it for you," Etheldra said through clenched teeth. "I did *not* travel all this way to come home to an inn full of *no* bread."

"Oh, it's all right, dear—" Earl tried, but Etheldra pushed his hand away.

"Bread. Tomorrow." She wagged her finger in Bev's face. "Or else."

She snatched up her plate and strode across the room.

"Goodness," Bev said with a laugh. "That's a bit extreme, even for Etheldra."

"I'm sorry. I think the heat's gotten to her," Earl said with a nervous chuckle. "She's been this way since we got back. More so than usual," he added with a smile. "I'm sure a good night's rest will set her right."

"I'll see about making the bread tomorrow," Bev said. "But if it's a mess, don't blame me. Blame the temperatures."

Gore Dewey, the blacksmith, was the next to walk in, saying he'd been too long in the hot forge, and Lillie was right behind him, with a similar complaint about the bakery oven.

"Understand completely," Bev said, gesturing to the food. "Plenty for everyone. Help yourself."

Gore plated his meal quickly, but Lillie lingered. "This looks delicious, Bev. I'm exhausted. Can barely look at another peach." She groaned as she saw the compote on the table. "Don't be mad at me if I skip that tonight."

"No hard feelings whatsoever," Bev said with a hearty laugh. "Allen tells me that you guys are overrun with solstice pie orders thanks to your cake-making skills at his wedding. Lots of peach pies, then?"

"Peach, blueberry, cherry, chocolate cream pie. Lemon curd and meringues. Fruit tarts. Galettes. Hand pies." She counted off her fingers. "Some of the orders didn't specify a filling, so at least that makes it somewhat easier." She sighed. "Good thing the farmers are having a banner year, or else we'd be in trouble."

"I went there myself," Bev said. "Outrageous how much they have." She pointed to the spinach on the table. "Alice practically begged me to take some. Can't believe she still has it this late in the season."

Lillie yawned and piled spinach onto her plate. "Well, I'm happy to eat it. Still haven't quite had my fill after five years—" She stopped, perhaps remembering there were strangers around. "Well, you know."

"I know." Bev nodded. "Go sit and eat then put your feet up. I daresay you've earned it."

Lillie did so, and Bev tidied the table mindlessly before making herself a plate. She hadn't been sure how it would all taste, but it was perhaps one of the better meals she'd made lately, if she did say so herself. The peaches were perfectly ripe, the sage beautifully fragrant, and the addition of the spinach was a perfect twist to the sweetness of the pork. All in all, Wim McKee would've been proud.

With her plate clean, Bev sat back on her stool and smiled as she remembered her old boss, the innkeeper who'd found her bleeding on his rosemary bush six years before. Things had changed around in Pigsend since he'd died, but she hoped he would've been happy to see the inn so well cared for. She hoped he would've even taken a liking to Biscuit, though he would've frowned upon the dog sleeping indoors.

And yet, you're trying to give it all up.

The voice was quiet, a little mean, but not entirely wrong. Bev had been digging into her past, trying to understand who she'd been before she'd arrived. It was a bit of self-preservation, as several queen's soldiers had come to town who'd been curious to the point of suspicion.

"That was divine," Solan said, rising with a bright smile. They brought their plate to Bev with a bow. "You are quite the wizard."

Bev started as Etheldra's sharp gaze turned to her. "Erm. Thank you. Just have some good recipes and great produce."

"The earth is silently humble," Solan said, as if reciting a piece of poetry, "but the sea's grandeur speaks for itself."

"Beautifully put," Bev said, taking the plate. "Let me know if there's anything else I can do for you this evening."

Something small and hard hit Bev's shin: Biscuit's tail. The laelaps watched the guest dreamily waltz up the stairs with something akin to hunger.

"Knock it off," Bev muttered to the laelaps.

Biscuit stared for a moment longer before dropping his gaze and putting his head on his paws once more. But his golden eyes were wide open.

"That's a beautiful dog you have," Feliciano said, bringing his plate. Stephen was right behind him, the two almost perfectly in sync. "What's his name?"

"Biscuit," Bev said. "Or Mr. Biscuit."

They shared a look and laughed. Stephen knelt beside Biscuit and held out his hand. "I do love dogs. They're such wonderful companions."

Biscuit gave his hand a sniff but didn't react otherwise.

"He's feeling a bit off lately," Bev said, reaching down to scratch Biscuit's ears. "Not sure if it's this heat or what."

"Oh, it's dreadful, isn't it?" Stephen said, rising. "I almost swooned on our way here, didn't I, Feli?"

"Took us three times as long to make the journey," his friend replied with a weary shake of his head. "Practically cried when the inn came into view."

"You didn't say what you were in town for," Bev said. "Just the solstice?"

They shared a look of concern, and Bev had a hunch she wouldn't get the truth out of them. "Yes. We've decided to stay until the temperature cools off a bit."

"You'll be here a long time yet," Etheldra said, bringing her plate up to Bev. "Gonna be ages before it breaks, you know. Not a cloud in the sky."

"The weather can be so fickle," Feliciano said. "We'll hopefully depart after a good summer storm."

Etheldra pursed her lips. "Strange for a pair of travelers to stay here. One would say suspicious—"

"Thank you, Etheldra," Bev said, a note of warning in her voice. There was nothing to be suspicious about, at least not that Bev was aware of. "I hear you've had a tough journey. I hope you get some good rest tonight."

Earl, who'd been around enough to know when Bev was dismissing them, joined his bride and offered Bev a bright smile. "I'm sure we will. We've got lots to do around the house, what with me moving in—"

"Harrumph. Didn't think this marriage through. Didn't know I'd have to give up my personal space," Etheldra grumbled as she left Earl by the front door.

Earl frowned, turning back to Bev. "I'm honestly not sure what's gotten into her. She was… Well, she was still Etheldra, but she was so happy on our trip. But since the moment we got back here, she's been nothing but sour." He turned to Feliciano and Stephen. "My apologies."

"Not to worry," Feliciano said.

"Have a good night, Earl," Bev said. "Hopefully, she'll be in better spirits tomorrow."

He nodded, thanked her for her understanding, and left. The rest of the diners seemed to be winding down, as well, though the sun was still bright outside.

"I think we'll take a walk," Stephen said. "Since it's still so nice out."

"Would you mind if I joined you?" Max asked. "This was such a good meal. I'm afraid I ate too much."

"I did, as well, but I've got to get back home.

Preparing for a trip to Queen's Capital in the morning," Bardoff said.

Bev didn't miss how both Feliciano and Stephen gave him a second look.

"Well, safe travels," Bev said. "Visiting old professors?"

He nodded. "It's been ages since I've been back. Thought it was time."

The four left together, along with Gore, which left Bev alone with Biscuit to tidy up. She left the food out, in case someone came late, and started scrubbing the pots and used plates. As she stood in the window and worked, she tried to look on the bright side of the season—at least it was still light out.

As the moments ticked on, and the sun dropped lower in the sky, a few more guests arrived, and soon Bev just had Vellora's commander's room left. But as she was checking in the last guests, the front door scraped open, and Vellora and a new man walked in.

"Hey, Bev," Vellora said, gesturing to him. "Meet my commander."

Chapter Three

Vellora's commander carried himself as if he were still commanding armies. Broad-shouldered, with dark skin and hair cut short against his scalp, he had a baritone voice that echoed in the space as he introduced himself.

"Andres Rade," he said, bowing slightly. "At your service."

"Welcome to the Weary Dragon, and Pigsend," Bev said with a smile she didn't quite feel. All the angst she'd had about meeting him wasn't resolved by looking him in the face. In fact, her trepidation was worse now that she was faced with *actually* asking him the questions she'd been mulling over for weeks now.

"Commander Rade," Vellora began, but Andres waved her off.

"Just Andres, Vellora, please. It's been six years since the war ended. I'm no one's commander now." He spoke warmly, but there was a tinge of sadness in his voice.

Vellora shifted as if she thought his title *was* necessary, but she cleared her throat and went on. "This is Bev, the keeper of the Weary Dragon." She looked around the dining room. "Erm…you do have a room available for my old commander, right?"

"Indeed I do," Bev said. "Room number five is all ready for you."

"Why don't I take your bag upstairs, and you can get something to eat?" Vellora said, picking up Andres's bag before he could say otherwise.

"How was your journey?" Bev said, trying for anything other than the elephant in the room. At least he didn't outright say he recognized her. That counted for something, she supposed.

"Long but not awful," he said, scanning the empty room. "Full house tonight?"

"Yes, everyone left a few minutes before you arrived," Bev said. "Please, help yourself to as much dinner as you want. Still a chance someone might come late, but more likely, you're the last to arrive."

"This looks delightful," he said, picking up one of the empty plates.

Bev couldn't help but watch him carefully. Did he have the secrets to her mysterious past locked away inside his bald head? She couldn't just come out with it this evening, not with so many ears around. Perhaps in the morning, when the travelers cleared out, she could sit down with him.

"I don't think I've ever had such a meal at an inn before," he said.

"The pork came from Vellora's shop," Bev said as Vellora came down the stairs. "Very fortunate to have her next door."

"We're the fortunate ones," Vellora said.

"Have some, Vellora," Bev said. "There's plenty left."

"Not often I'm on this side of your meals." Vellora gave an eager smile. "I can't tell you the number of nights I go to bed salivating over the smells coming out of your kitchen."

"Well, you should come over," Bev said. "Goodness knows there's plenty of room."

"My wife might take offense," Vellora said. "As I'm supposed to be eating her cooking every night."

Bev ducked a smile, and Vellora joined her old commander at the table. It was clear the butcher still held Andres in high regard, deferring to him in both word and mannerism. Andres, to his credit, seemed comfortable in her presence and eventually, Vellora relaxed. For as much as the commander was here to answer Bev's questions, it seemed they genuinely enjoyed each other's company, and Bev was happy he'd made the trip for Vellora's sake.

"Where did you say you traveled from?" Bev asked.

"I live in the south still," he said. "Keep up with my best soldiers. The ones who want to hear from me, in any case. Some of 'em don't want to, and that's fine. They've got their lives to live, and we're all fortunate the queen lets us do that."

"For the moment," Vellora muttered darkly.

"We're happy to have Vellora here in Pigsend," Bev said. "I know Ida's happy she rolled into town."

"Yes, I don't think I've heard that story," Andres said with a look at Vellora. "I seem to remember you swearing up and down you'd never get married."

"Well, as it so happens, I ended up in Pigsend," Vellora said. "Trying to find my place in the world. Ended up here at the Weary Dragon for a night."

"I do remember that," Bev said with a smile.

"The next day, as I was packing up to leave, I see the most beautiful woman across the street. And she's carrying a whole pig across her shoulders. Bigger than she was, and to her, it was light as air."

Andres furrowed his brow but didn't say anything.

Vellora was lost in her own memories and didn't notice. "In any case, I asked Bev about her and found an excuse to stay. Then another, and another. Eventually, I drummed up the nerve to ask her to the tea shop in town—"

"I think she asked you, didn't she?" Bev said. "She was eyeing you as much as you were eyeing her."

"Well, however it happened, it did, and I'm so grateful for it." Vellora's pale cheeks had gone pink as she grinned. "She's the best thing that ever happened to me."

"I'm happy you're happy," Andres said.

Bev couldn't have agreed more, but as the clock chimed eight, she decided to leave them to catching up and continue the evening's chores. She was avoiding the inevitable, but she needed more time to think about what she wanted to ask him. How did one come out and ask, "Do you know anything about wizards who served the king, and am I one of them?" And what would she do if he had the answer? Nothing, she told herself. So why was she digging? Because she needed to find out before someone else did.

She blew air between her lips, ignoring Biscuit's whines as he scraped at the door.

"Leave them be," Bev said.

She finished the dishes she could and found herself still full of nervous energy. She turned to the unused bread starter on the counter, reminded of Etheldra's warning. Well, she could give it a go and see. She'd have to shorten the rise time, keep it in the root cellar, perhaps bake it first thing in the morning. But perhaps she could do something tonight, when the temperatures were cooler.

"Fine."

She got out her ingredients—flour, barm, rosemary, water, and salt—and assembled them as she'd done a thousand times before. The work was relaxing, easing the tension in her shoulders. Something somewhat predictable, even if the timing wasn't. Biscuit rested next to her as she worked, his golden eyes fixed on her. When the dough was ready, she tossed a tea towel over it and brought it to the root cellar.

"Etheldra can't be mad at me if it doesn't turn out," Bev said with a chuckle. "We did try, didn't we, Biscuit?"

He let out a low ruff.

She crossed the yard, once again amazed that the sun hadn't even thought about setting yet, but stopped short when she got to the kitchen. Andres stood there, examining her drying herbs with interest. When he heard her footsteps, he turned with a bright smile.

"Evening, Ms. Bev. I hope you don't mind the intrusion, but Vellora said I might find you in here." He put his hands in his pockets. "I believe you and I need to chat."

Bev's throat went dry. "Yes, we do." She gestured to the kitchen table. "Erm. Have a seat. Should be private enough in here."

"Vellora tells me one never knows who's coming and going around here," he said as he crossed the kitchen to take a seat. "Lots of strangers who may be holding secrets."

"That's certainly true."

Bev moved her stool to sit, but before she could, Biscuit appeared from beneath the table, putting both paws on Andres's legs and unfurling his tongue in greeting.

"Is this…" Andres eyed her. "A laelaps?"

"Good eye," Bev said. "To everyone else, he's a dog. Arrived here in town last fall and decided he liked this place. The *second* of many curiosities that have happened around here, leading me to believe there's something afoot."

Andres nodded. "Why don't you start at the beginning?"

Bev told him the story of finding the first amulet piece in the garden when there'd been a spate of sinkholes, and how she thought it might've been what the soldiers who'd caused the earthquakes had been looking for. Then, after Biscuit arrived, finding the second one in the thicket down the road and having a terrible vision she'd later come to know as the Battle of Eriwall.

"I haven't a clue if these visions are mine," Bev said. "Or if they're connected to the amulet itself. For a while, I'd convinced myself of the latter, but I hear laelaps only affiliate to the powerful magical sort, so..." She chuckled, looking down at Biscuit. "Perhaps not."

"Where is the amulet now?"

"It's, erm..." She trusted him to discuss the amulet, but not quite enough to give up the secret of Lower Pigsend. "I met a wizard. He identified the amulet as a wizard's helper, and...well, it was better in his hands than mine, especially with all the soldiers who pass through town."

"I don't doubt it," Andres said.

"I was hoping you might know something about wizards who had that kind of amulet, who might've been at the Battle of Eriwall, and...well, I don't know, tell me if you recognize me or know who I am?" Bev finished with a half-smile, feeling quite silly when it was all out in the open.

He surveyed her for a moment. "Before I answer, why do you want to know?"

"What do you mean?"

He gestured to the inn. "This place is safe. Well-loved, clearly. Vellora says you're a staple of the community. Why are you eager to uncover a past that wants to stay buried?"

"Because I'm not the only one interested," Bev said. "There've been a few soldiers in town who've been more than a little curious, and I worry one of them's going to find the truth before I do. Better to be prepared, you know?" She stopped, tilting her head. "I don't look familiar, do I?"

"Can't say that you do," he said with a low chuckle. "The king employed many different kinds of magic users: wizards, mages, witches—basically anyone with magic wanted to fight for him. There was a group of wizards at the Battle of Eriwall, the King's Quartet. They had amulets that improved magical abilities as you've described. It is *possible* you could be one of them, or that amulet you found was."

The name didn't ring a bell, but Bev wasn't surprised about that. "What happened to them?"

"You don't want to know," he said warily. "But they're gone now. If you were one of them, you're better off not knowing."

"Why?"

He swallowed hard. "That battle was…difficult. Lots of decisions were made. Political ones, which took more life than was probably necessary." He seemed to be considering his words. "The Battle of Eriwall was a turning point. But not because we lost the battle. Because we lost the hearts and minds of the people."

"How?"

Once again, his words were measured. "The kingside army was filled with magical users. Not all of them were of the purest hearts, so to speak. They took things too far. The queen was able to show the people, who far outnumbered those with magic, that allowing such creatures to have free rein wasn't safe.

Lots of folks who'd been waiting for the battle to play out finally landed on her side." He let out a low breath. "Even with all our power, we were overwhelmed. Especially when key magic users defected, giving her the tools she needed to defeat us."

It was quite the epic tale. "You said I'm better off not knowing if I was one of those elite wizards. Why?"

"Because they were the ones who caused the most damage," he said softly. "And the most prized targets of the queen. She and her henchmen made sure every one of those wizards was destroyed—because they're the ones who could rise up and defeat her."

Bev sucked in a breath. "Defeat her? Who in the world would want to do that?"

He gave her a sympathetic smile. "There are *whispers* that some of the magic folk, obviously not the wizards, but lesser mages who escaped the purge, want to overthrow the queen. Start the war all over again."

"No." While Bev obviously didn't remember anything about the time before Pigsend, she'd spoken to enough folks to know no one wanted to revisit that horrible time.

He nodded. "Not saying they're going to be successful at it, but the more I travel, the more I hear of people having secret meetings all over the place. If you ask me, that's probably why you've seen so many soldiers around lately. They're trying to stamp out the remnants of magical users so they don't have a chance to, erm, *talk*."

"I haven't heard anything about that around here," Bev said. "But I doubt anyone would tell me anything anyway."

"I hear you've got quite a knack for finding things out," he said. "Vellora tells me you saved her and her wife from a spot of trouble with a blackmailer—among other things."

"Not sure how I keep getting pulled into these adventures," Bev said, pushing air between her lips. "But I'm glad to help, in any case." She rose. "I've got to finish up here. Is there anything else you can think of that might help me?"

"Yes." He chuckled. "Stop digging. You're better off forgetting any past that had something to do with magic or wizards' amulets. Whoever you were is gone. You're Bev, proprietor of the Weary Dragon. That's all anyone needs to know about you."

"But—"

Before she could finish, the front door opened once more. Bev waited to hear voices, but there were none. She shared a curious look with Andres before rising. "Is someone there?"

"Bev? Are you back there?"

Bev's heart sank as she hurried out into the front room. She recognized that voice, the face, the uniform. He smiled at her warmly, hopefully innocent of the conversation she'd had with Andres in the other room.

"Zed," Bev said, a little breathlessly. Allen's father was a *very* high-ranking soldier in the queen's army, though he had been nice enough during the wedding festivities. "I'm so sorry, but I'm full up right now. I don't have a room—"

He waved her off. "No need. I was patrolling town and thought I'd stop in for a spot of dinner. Though it seems I should've come earlier. Silly me. Thought with the solstice coming, you might push dinner to a later hour. But it seems like I missed most of it."

"I'm so sorry about that. If I'd known, I would've saved you some," Bev said, willing her pulse to return to normal. "Does Allen know you're back?"

His gaze swept the room as if he were looking for someone. "Not yet. Knocked on his door, but he didn't answer. Probably asleep. Those bakers, they get up so early."

"Especially now," Bev said. "Apparently, he and Lillie are busier than ever making solstice pies."

"Oh, I'd love a solstice pie," he said with a wistful smile as he sat at the table. "I—"

His face darkened immediately as if his mortal enemy had walked into the room. Bev followed his gaze to where Andres stood in the kitchen doorway.

"What are *you* doing here?" they said in unison.

Chapter Four

"Erm, you two know each other?" Bev asked, though the question was mostly rhetorical. She'd never seen two people stare at each other with more animosity, each willing the other to burst into flames.

"The better question is why is this monster defiling Pigsend?" Zed shot back. "Keep your distance, Bev, lest you find yourself on the wrong end of a spear."

"I'd say the same for you, filthy turncoat," Andres snarled.

"Turncoat?" Zed took a step forward.

"All right, all right," Bev said, holding up her hands. "What are you doing back in town, anyway?"

"There's lots of activity around the solstice," Zed said, his narrow gaze never leaving Andres. "Folks out on the roads, causing trouble to commemorate the end of the war. Her Majesty's asked her soldiers to fan out and keep an eye on things. I offered to take this area." He nodded at Andres. "Clearly, it's a good thing I did."

"A soldier of your *ranking*, taking a position in the sticks?" Andres snorted. "Seems unlikely."

"The sticks happen to be where I grew up," Zed replied with a glare. "My son actually lives and works across the street. He's the baker."

"The one who won't talk with you?"

"That's enough," Bev said as Zed took a step toward Andres. "Now if the two of you don't have anything civil to say, you won't be saying it. Zed, I do apologize, but there's no more dinner nor is there a bed for you, so I think your business is concluded. You're welcome to try again tomorrow, if you need."

"Might just have to do that," Zed said. "It's clear that I need a bigger presence in town to keep an eye on troublemakers."

"The only troublemaker here is *you*," Andres said with a sneer. "I'm here visiting a friend. It's not illegal to travel, is it?"

Zed glared at him. "Not unless you're traveling for something nefarious."

"I'm sure—" Bev began, but clearly, she wasn't a part of this conversation.

Andres waved his arm. "I check in with my registrar yearly, sign my forms. Not that *you'd* know anything about that."

"You're right, because I picked the winning side," Zed said.

Andres took another step forward. "You betrayed your countrymen."

"The countrymen betrayed themselves," Zed replied, also taking a step.

Now the men were within striking distance of one another, and Bev wasn't sure she knew how to stop them. She held her breath, waiting for the other to hit first. But they only stared at each other, teeth bared and fists clenched. The clock on the wall chimed, and both men jumped.

"I'm going back to camp," Zed said to Bev. "Keep an eye on him for me."

"I'm sure I won't need to—"

"It's *you* she should keep an eye on," Andres said, though he seemed less keen on throwing punches now. "But if you need me, I'll be spending time with my dear friend across the street. As long as that isn't a crime."

Zed sniffed and spun on his heel, walking toward the door. He paused and looked over his shoulder once more. "You'll see us tomorrow, Bev. Have a good night."

~

For both their sakes, Bev hoped Zed and Andres

didn't cross paths again. There didn't seem to be any benefit to it, other than sniping at one another. Bev sincerely doubted Andres was in town for anything other than answering Bev's questions and spending time with Vellora. Zed hadn't struck her as the sort of fellow who'd fly off the handle, either, so whatever bad blood existed between them probably ran deep. Too deep for a simple innkeeper to fix. Better they left each other alone.

Still, the conversations the night before had given her lots to think about. She'd never thought about anyone, least of all former soldiers, wanting to band together to overthrow the queen. It seemed the sort of thing someone far away from Pigsend might do, and the idea of a rebellion of any kind brewing in her small town made her tired. The folks around here were too focused on their industries; after all, who could foment insurrection when there were peaches to pick?

But she'd be naive to think she'd *never* crossed paths with anyone with those kinds of thoughts in mind. The inn was the temporary home to all sorts of travelers. While the folks who'd served the queen were up front about their employer to varying degrees, the folks who'd served the king seemed less so. She knew about Vellora, of course, but it had taken years for the other butcher to mention her participation in the war.

More importantly, it seemed Andres wasn't the

fellow to tell Bev more about herself. She'd been hoping the mention of amulets and wizards' helpers would jog his memory, and he'd…well, she'd rather hoped he'd come out with a full tale. Instead, she'd gotten a whole bunch of nothing.

Her mind was full of these thoughts as she tended to her chores. But as she walked to the stable, her gaze landed on her garden, and her brows rose. She'd pruned the unwieldy herbs the day before, cutting most of them down close to the ground. But now, the garden had returned with a vengeance, almost *taller* than the day before.

"Goodness," Bev said, putting her hand to her head. "Well, suppose I can cut it back again."

But before she could tend to that, Sin, Bev's old mule, brayed unhappily from the stables. Bev returned to her original task and tended to her beast, refreshing her water and hay.

"Sorry for the delay, old girl," Bev said, patting her on the nose. "You wouldn't believe what my garden looks like right now."

Sin brayed, as if she couldn't care less.

"Right. Let me see if I can't find you an apple."

She left the stable and found Biscuit sitting in front of the herb garden, his nose pointed in the air and his tail wagging so fast it caused a little dust cloud on the ground. His gaze seemed to be locked on the rosemary plant, which towered over everything. Bev had to give the laelaps credit; she'd told him once never to touch her garden, and he was still adhering to that command all these months later.

She snapped off a branch of rosemary and looked at him. "Are you dying for a piece?"

He lifted his head, as if agreeing with her.

"This *one* time. You can have some." She held it out. "But only this *one* time, understand?"

He snatched the rosemary from her hand and gobbled it up. She waited for him to go for seconds, but he listened.

"Come on," Bev said, breaking off another piece to dry in the window. "Let's go check on that bread and get Sin an apple."

The root cellar was dark and cool—at least cooler than the early morning around them. Bev peered at her bread, finding it risen and ready for shaping. Typically, that was a task reserved for mid-afternoon, so she could get the bread in the oven around four.

"I'll be baking these before noon at this rate," Bev said to Biscuit, who was inspecting the crate of potatoes nearby. "Suppose Etheldra will have to settle for cold bread instead of no bread at all. But that'll be all right. What's life without a little variety?"

Bev procured the apple for Sin and returned to the kitchen, though there wasn't really much for her to do until the guests left for the day. So she settled on her stool at the front desk, Biscuit perched next to her, and waited, her mind whirring with thoughts about Zed and Andres and why they might be so angry with one another. Zed had told her he used to be a kingside soldier, but he'd changed his stripes toward the end of the war. That certainly seemed like a reason for Andres to be cross with him, but why would Zed be cross with Andres?

She tapped her fingers on the front desk, peering through the windows at the bakery across the street. Regardless of why Zed was in town, Bev would need to give Lillie a heads-up. When Zed had been staying at the inn during Allen's not-wedding, he hadn't suspected the pobyd of being anything more than his son's assistant. But if he knew the truth, she'd be arrested for illegal use of magic. It was a miracle Zed hadn't noticed the wedding cake had been full of it.

At a quarter to seven, Allen arrived with a basket of blueberry muffins that smelled divine, even from a distance.

"Morning, Bev—" He stopped short. "What's wrong?"

"How can you tell?" Bev asked.

"You've got that look about you." He crossed the room. "What's going on?"

Bev told him about Zed, and his face fell. "He told me he was headed back to Queen's Capital after the wedding."

Bev nodded. "He said he'd been given new orders. The queen wants soldiers patrolling the country during the solstice and so close to the anniversary." She glanced at the stairs, where Andres and the others were still sleeping. "Supposedly, people get ornery. Cause trouble."

"Not around here, they don't," Allen said. "Unless you count Earl's fireworks causing too much of a stir." He shook his head. "Something else is up. It always seems to be with him."

Bev briefly told him about Vellora's commander and their angry encounter the night before. "It seems they've got history. Zed was practically ready to arrest Andres for standing there."

"Why is Vellora's commander in town, anyway?" Allen asked, rubbing the back of his neck. "Not that my father should be arresting anyone."

"Vellora invited him to talk with me," Bev said, a little nervously. "About my past. If he had any information about it or knew who I was or where I came from."

Allen's brow furrowed. "Did he?"

"Not really. He told me that the past is better off staying buried," Bev said. "But he mentioned there were people who wanted to overthrow the queen. Can you imagine?"

"I can. Especially people like Lillie," Allen said.

Bev inhaled the steam from the muffins then blinked. They almost smelled *too* good. "Did Lillie make these?"

"Yeah, why?" Allen asked.

Bev plucked one out of the basket and popped a piece into her mouth. Instantly, the sweet taste of blueberries, the tart zing of lemon, and the sweetness of sugar exploded on her tongue. She chewed thoughtfully and gave Allen a look. "She shouldn't be using her magic."

"She didn't." He broke a piece off the muffin and ate it. The sensations seemed to hit him the same, and he shook his head. "She's not *supposed* to. She knows better." He sniffed the basket. "Maybe this wasn't the right basket. She was making a couple of batches this morning. I think she was planning to take one to, erm, the other place."

Lillie had been booted from Lower Pigsend a few months before for almost breaking the charm that kept its inhabitants safe from the queen's soldiers. It had been an act of desperation, one that she often expressed regret over, and she'd been taking produce, gold, and baked goods to leave on Merv's doorstep as an act of contrition.

"Goodness, glad you caught that before we really made a mistake," Allen said.

"She probably shouldn't be taking any trips down there, what with your father camped up north." Bev chuckled. "Besides that, didn't you say you were overrun with orders? How do you have time to make extras?"

"If you're already baking muffins, it's not that hard to make a double recipe," he said with a shrug. "But you're right. We've got to be more careful until he moves on." He paused, looking at Bev. "You don't think Zed is here to arrest Lillie, do you? Maybe he tasted her magic on the wedding cake."

It was certainly possible. "Just tell her to keep a low profile. I'll try to figure out what he's doing in town for real in the meantime." She chuckled. "Maybe I'll make him a solstice pie to get him talking. He did mention he'd missed those."

"Well, let me know if you need a recipe," Allen said, picking up the basket. "I'll be back in a bit with more muffins."

~

Allen returned with muffins and an apology from Lillie, who was mortified the wrong muffins got sent over. The second batch was delicious, though not quite as mind-bogglingly as the first. But all the guests enjoyed them, including Andres, who stopped to apologize for the argument the night before.

"I'm so sorry you were caught in the middle of that," he said, as Stephen and Feliciano walked out the door, deep in conversation. "I wasn't expecting to see *him*, of all people, here in Pigsend."

"It's quite all right. I wasn't expecting to see him either," Bev said with a chuckle. "But it seems you've got history."

"You can say that again." Andres took another muffin. "You said his son baked these?"

"His son and Lillie, his assistant," Bev said.

"Probably should check them for poison, then," Andres said.

"Oh, Allen's not..." Bev wasn't sure how much information to share. "They're fine."

"Apple fell far from the tree, then?" He took another bite, sighing with satisfaction. "You know, Zed and I used to be good friends. That's why his betrayal was so much harder to bear."

"He switched sides, right?" Bev said.

Andres nodded. "It was right after that battle we were talking about last night. I'm not saying what we did was right, but... Well, it didn't sit well with him. So he took all his knowledge to the commanders on the other side in exchange for immunity—including how the queen's soldiers could defeat the mages and wizards at the king's disposal."

Bev blinked. No wonder he'd risen so fast in the queen's ranks—and that Andres was so angry with him. "That sounds like an awful betrayal."

Andres nodded. "It took us all by surprise. Zed knew all our most closely guarded secrets. And to see him now, walking around with his medals as if he earned them by valor instead of..." He finished the muffin, chewing thoughtfully. "I think it's better if he keeps his distance. I'm not sure I can be civil."

"Did Vellora know him?" Bev asked. The butcher hadn't seemed to when he'd been in town last.

"No. She was one of my soldiers. Zed was at my level, with his own legion at his command. And every one of them ended up..." He forced his lips into a smile. "This conversation is quite dark for such a lovely day. I know Vellora wanted to show me around the countryside today. Might as well get to it."

"Steer clear of the northern fields," Bev said. To Andres's confused look, she said, "That's where Zed said he was staying."

"Ah. Good idea."

He turned to walk toward the door, but before he could get there, the front door burst open, and Zed stormed in, flanked by three soldiers, all wearing furious expressions.

"You!" Zed cried, pointing his sword at Andres. "You're under arrest!"

"For *what*?" Andres cried.

"For destroying the queen's property," Zed said. "And releasing our horses!"

Chapter Five

"You're out of your mind," Andres said. "First of all, I haven't been anywhere *near* your camp. And second, what in the world would I do with horses?"

"They were in the pen last night," Zed said. "This morning, they're gone."

"Did one of your soldiers leave the gate open?" Andres asked with a smirk. "Seems like the sort of thing a lazy leader would allow to happen."

"The gate was locked," one of the other soldiers said. "We wouldn't be so careless."

"Wouldn't you?" Andres crossed his arms. "Seems like instead of standing here wanting to arrest me, you should be scouring the countryside for your missing property."

"Got that covered. But I wanted to make sure I got you in irons before you caused any more trouble."

"Now hang on a second," Bev said, holding up her hands. "Zed, you know I'm keen on finding the truth, but Andres has been here all morning. When could he have possibly—"

"Last night," Zed said. "I doubt you keep that close an eye on your guests. He could've easily slipped out in the night, released our horses—"

"Through a locked pen?" Andres chuckled. "I'm not that good."

"And come back," Zed finished. "In any case, we're holding you until we locate our property."

"I'm not really one to argue with the law," Bev said. "But it seems like you're jumping to conclusions here, Zed. Maybe we should all take a breath. Why don't I come with you and see about finding those horses? We had a spate of animals go wandering off during the Harvest Festival. I probably know of some spots we can look."

"As long as he comes with us," Zed said, pointing at Andres.

"No handcuffs, as he's not been proven guilty yet," Bev said. "But sure. Andres, why don't you join us? More eyes are better anyway."

Andres seemed put out by the idea but didn't argue. Bev walked alongside Zed, who kept throwing angry glances at Andres. Biscuit, who'd been very interested when the soldiers had arrived, walked beside her, his golden eyes darting around. She was grateful the laelaps had snapped out of his frenzy to come help; something told her his keen nose would be needed.

As the group marched through town, they spread out a bit, with Zed's two soldiers flanking Andres and Bev and Zed breaking out ahead. When they were far enough to be out of earshot, Bev leaned over to mutter to Zed, "Why would Andres want to steal your horses?"

"I can think of several hundred reasons," he said darkly. "He's not a good person, Bev. His history is sordid, and his hands are bloody. I don't think it's wise to take his side. Whatever he's doing—"

"Visiting Vellora," Bev said lightly. She left out the part about him answering questions about her past, of course. "It's all innocent, I promise."

"That's the story he told you, but I've got my suspicions. How he's managed to avoid arrest is beyond me." Zed cast his foe another glare. "The things he did in the war were horrific. Can't believe he can sleep at night."

He said much the same about you, Bev thought. "What sorts of things?"

"I don't want to offend your delicate sensibilities," Zed said.

"I'm not that delicate," Bev said with a look.

"Suffice to say, he earned his title as the Butcher

of Eriwall," Zed said. "Seeing him in action there was so abhorrent to me...I had no choice but to take what I knew to the queen to stop him. Otherwise, *I* wouldn't have been able to live with myself."

It seemed the flip side of the same coin. Bev supposed that was common in war.

"He mentioned that battle to me," Bev said, measuring her words. "That it was full of decisions that he made for the greater good."

"That's what he says," Zed said with a grimace. "That's not what happened."

"What did happen?"

"It was a good example of why magical people shouldn't be allowed to run roughshod across the rest of us." Zed looked back at Andres. "Once I decided they'd taken things too far, I gathered what I knew about their weaknesses and took it to the queen. I feared if I didn't, those with unchecked power would continue to lord over the rest of us."

"You seem very concerned about that," Bev said. "You must've seen some awful things. But is it worth the total ban on magical creatures? Surely, there's got to be a middle ground."

"With magical creatures, there never is. They'll take and take until before you know it, you're..." He sighed.

"Still, a sordid history doesn't a horse thief make," Bev said. "Just because you've had differences in the past doesn't mean there's reason to accuse him without proof now. Andres doesn't have magic, does he?"

"Well, no."

"Then how could he be responsible?" Bev asked.

Zed made a face, as if there was more he wanted to say, but he remained quiet as the group came to the large open field north of town, where the Harvest Festival held the judging contest for the livestock. Now it was dotted with several white tents and a single empty pen—smaller than the one used in the fall—that sat off to the side. From the haphazard way the grass had been cut, it was clear a group of horses had been kept there for a short period of time and hadn't finished grazing on the field.

"Well?" Zed crossed his arms over his chest. "Where are they?"

Bev walked to the pen. The gate was shut, but not locked, and there weren't any hoofprints or signs that the horses had jumped the fence. They looked like they had just...disappeared.

"I'm sure there's a logical explanation," Bev said, looking down at Biscuit, who was sniffing the ground as she walked.

"They probably got spooked by something." Andres gestured toward the nearby tents. "Why didn't any of your soldiers notice? Horses don't disappear without a sound."

"Why don't you tell us?" Zed shot back. "Magic is your area of expertise."

He scoffed. "Magic? I don't have any magic, Zed."

"You know how to get it. To use it." Zed smirked. "To hurt people with it. And you clearly have friends with magic."

"Not anymore, thanks to you," Andres retorted. "Or did you forget what happened—"

Bev cleared her throat loudly before the two came to blows. "Okay, let's see what Biscuit can find, eh? He's got a good nose. I'm sure if we split up, we can find—"

But Biscuit had already slipped under the fence. His tail was curled up behind him, his nose pressed to the ground as he sniffed around. Bev leaned on the fence post, waiting for him to pick up the scent of the horses, but he kept circling the same spot.

"What's he doing?" one of the soldiers asked Bev.

"Not sure," Bev said, rubbing the back of her neck. "He has been acting funny lately. Maybe he's still not feeling right." She put her hands to her mouth. "Biscuit! Have you scented the horses yet?"

Biscuit stopped then promptly sat on the ground and stared at her.

"This is ridiculous," Zed said. "He's a dog. He probably smelled some leftover meat or something."

"Just give me a moment," Bev said, hopping the

fence. "Biscuit? What is it?"

Biscuit unfurled his tongue and smiled at her, his tail wagging against the grass. Bev knelt beside him, scratching his face. She'd long ago learned that it was better to trust the laelaps, as he tended to know more than she did, but she couldn't help but wonder if he *was* a bit off his rocker at the moment.

"What is it?" Bev repeated, looking around.

Biscuit lowered his nose to the ground, sniffing a plump, green caterpillar on a leaf.

"Oh, goodness me, Biscuit." Bev whispered. "You can't possibly... Andres is in real trouble if we don't locate those horses. Can't you give me something?"

Biscuit sniffed the caterpillar again, causing the creature to cling to the blade of grass.

Bev was about to call it when she noticed strange markings on the back of the caterpillar. When she tilted her head, it almost looked like...a saddle. And around the mouth, too, markings that almost resembled reins.

"Biscuit, are these the horses?" Bev asked, spotting more caterpillars inching along the ground.

Biscuit let out a low ruff.

"Erm, Zed," Bev called back to the soldiers, who were advancing on Andres. "How many horses did you say you had?"

Zed stopped, a bewildered look on his face. "Five. Why? Do you see them?"

"Come here for a moment. And watch your step." Zed crossed the pasture to stand next to her, and Bev carefully picked up a caterpillar. "What do you think this looks like?"

"A bug."

"Look closer." She lifted the caterpillar higher.

His frown deepened. "Stay here. I'll be right back."

He left her there, crossing the field and finding his tent. He ducked inside for only a moment then returned with a wooden chest. Andres seemed to know exactly what it was, but Bev had never seen it before. With the crate held gingerly, he climbed over the fence and came to kneel next to Bev.

He unlocked the chest, using a small key from around his neck, and revealed an assortment of vials holding different colored liquids. Bev recognized them as similar to one he'd used to undo the curse on Vicky's bracelet a few weeks ago. He pulled one from the back, examining it closely before turning to the first caterpillar.

"Put it down," he instructed.

Bev put the caterpillar down, and Zed poured a few drops of the potion onto its back. The creature stopped, as if frozen by magic, then began to contort and twist on the ground.

"Stand back," Zed said.

Bev rose to her feet, and not a moment too soon, because with a loud *pop* the caterpillar exploded into a large, dark brown horse wearing a saddle and reins. It nickered loudly, tossing its head as it presumably shook off the magic that had trapped it in such a small creature's body.

"Goodness," Bev said. "How did you do that?"

"Watch yourself," Zed said.

One by one, he added the potion to the caterpillars, and they returned to their horse shape. Each one earned a cry of surprise from the gathered soldiers, who watched the whole episode with wide eyes. When the last horse had regained its shape, Zed put a cork in the bottle and put it back into the chest, locking it tightly and picking it back up.

"How did you know those were the horses?" Zed asked, his tone strange.

"Biscuit's got a good nose," Bev said, hoping she wouldn't have to explain what he really was. "I asked him to find the horses, and he'd found them here."

"Mm." Zed turned, his gaze back on Andres, who'd hopped the fence along with Zed's soldiers as soon as the horses started appearing.

"Well, you found your horses," Andres said. "May I go now, since there hasn't been a crime committed?"

"I think there has," Zed said. "As you know, this sort of dangerous magic is outlawed by Her Majesty." Zed cracked a grin. "Andres Rade, you're under arrest for the illegal use of magic."

~

Bev did try to argue with Zed but was summarily escorted back to the inn by two of his soldiers.

"You'd be safer at your inn," one of the two soldiers, named Ollie, said. "At least until we've got everything under control."

"I daresay you've got it all under control," Bev said with a glare. "The horses have been found. There's no need for all this."

"The queen's property was transfigured by magic," the other soldier, Casimir, said, his eyes wide. "That's a capital offense."

Bev pursed her lips. Perhaps not the best time to be arguing. "Very well. I'll stay here at the inn like a good little innkeeper. But please tell Zed he owes me an explanation. And he needs more than a few spelled caterpillars to arrest Andres."

Zed seemed to know that as well, because around midday, he returned to the inn and demanded to know which room Andres was staying in.

"Why do you need to know?" Bev said.

"He's under arrest," Zed said. "I need to search his room."

"And what if you don't find anything incriminating?" Bev asked. "Will you let him go?"

"I'll find something." He glowered at her. "But on the off chance I don't, yes."

As a rule, Bev didn't let the law search rooms—she didn't even do it herself if she could help it—but she was confident Andres didn't have any magic. So she brought her universal key up to room five and opened the door. Inside, Andres's small suitcase was open, revealing a change of clothes and a spare set of boots. Zed made a beeline for the bag and rifled through it, throwing Andres's clothes unceremoniously on the floor. When he didn't find anything there, he moved on to the bedding, and began kicking the floor in search of a floorboard.

"What's all this noise?" Solan walked by, patting their ears. "What's this? A soldier? Searching the inn?"

"Just this room," Zed said with a too-calm expression. "We've got reason to believe the man staying here is dealing with illegal magic."

"Oh, goodness me, what a thing to do," Solan said with a gasp. "But if you would be so kind as to ransack the room quietly, I'm trying to get a few minutes of a nap. Late night, you know. That moon is so loud."

"What do you—"

Bev cleared her throat, glaring at Zed.

"Fine." Zed cleared his throat. "Enjoy the quiet."

"Thank you." Solan spun on their heel and walked back to their room.

"Are you satisfied?" Bev asked, her voice low.

"No magic in here. Andres didn't do it."

Zed sniffed, glancing around the room as if making triply sure he hadn't missed anything. "Fine. He's free to go. But he'd better stick around, or we'll think he's up to something."

"Since he hasn't gotten a chance to visit with his friend, I'm sure he'll want to do that before he continues on his way," Bev said. "And I do expect you to put his things back the way you found them, too. It's bad enough you scared the poor man by arresting him without cause."

"I doubt he thought twice about it," Zed said, throwing the clothes back in the bag without much care.

"We may not be fancy here in Pigsend, but we do follow the law," Bev said. "And if I hear of you harassing my guest without cause again, I'll have no choice but to ask Sheriff Rustin to intercede."

Rustin wouldn't do anything; in fact, Bev was fairly sure Zed outranked him in the grand scheme of things. Not to mention the local sheriff wasn't the sharpest tool in the shed. But the threat worked, and Zed nodded, begrudgingly.

"Very well. We'll leave him be." He lifted his finger. "But rest assured, we *will* find whoever's illegally using magic in this town. Even if I have to go door to door and test everyone myself."

Chapter Six

There were several reasons Zed going door to door would be terrible for the people of Pigsend—and not only because of Lillie. Ida Witzel, Etheldra, and a few others had some *sprinklings* of magic in their veins. Would it be enough to show up on whatever test Zed could concoct? Bev didn't know and didn't want to find out.

Andres returned to the inn, looking affronted and annoyed, but proclaiming he wasn't going to be bullied into cutting his trip short. To be safe, Bev walked him across the street to the butchery, where Vellora welcomed them up to her small apartment over the shop.

"If you don't mind keeping your voices down.

Ida's not feeling well," Vellora said, walking out with a plate of cookies from Allen's bakery. "I think the heat's getting to her."

"Poor dear," Bev said as Andres took a seat at the small table. "I think the heat's getting to everyone."

Andres snorted. "Not to Zed. He's always been that way."

"I'm glad they didn't hold you indefinitely," Bev said. "I don't have much sway, but what little I had seemed to work"

"And that's appreciated," Andres said with a nod as Vellora watched with a steely expression. "In my experience, the queen's soldiers have treated me more unfairly than most. The wounds we opened in the war are slow to close."

Bev burned with more questions, especially about Zed's accusations that Andres had been too vague with his history, but it was better to let sleeping dogs lie. After all, what good would it do?

"I do wonder what happened, though," Bev said, looking at Vellora. "How do horses turn into caterpillars?"

"Magic," Vellora said.

"Well, obviously," Bev said with a chuckle.

"Better to keep our noses out of it. Last thing we want is Zed looking too closely at Ida," Vellora said.

"Your wife is magical?" Andres asked.

Vellora nodded. "Descended from dryads. She's always had supernatural strength, but she never really thought too much about where it came from until we had that trouble with the blackmailer a few months ago. Etheldra Daws, who's Ida's grandmother's cousin, provided a bit of family history."

"And nobody's ever said anything to you about it?" Andres asked.

Vellora shook her head. "Etheldra says that the lineage is so far removed that the queen's folk won't find it interesting."

"Depends on the queen's folk, you know," Andres said. "I've seen soldiers arrest apothecaries who use a bit too much lavender."

"Zed's not one of those, is he?" Bev said.

"He's proven himself eager to do whatever it takes to save his own skin," Andres said before shaking his head. "But let's put this nasty business behind us. Bev, I think I'll lie low here at the Witzels' until this evening, if that's all right. Maybe you can leave me a plate?"

"I'd be happy to," Bev said, rising. "I've got to get back to the inn and check on things. Are you sure you're all right, Andres?"

"I'm with friends," he said with a bright smile. "I'm never better."

~

The excitement took up most of the morning, so the rosemary bread in the root cellar was almost overproofed by the time she got to it. She fired up the oven quickly and put the tins in before they got any higher. The bread would be cold by this evening, but at least it would be there.

In the meantime, Bev washed the guests' sheets from the night before and reset those rooms. With Stephan and Feliciano in one room, Solan in another, and Andres in room five, there were four openings for potential guests.

One of those rooms was taken around one in the afternoon, when a man with warm brown skin and dark hair gathered in a single braid came to stay. He introduced himself as Kemp Abora, and paid up-front to stay through the solstice.

"My grandfather used to say it was bad luck to travel during the solstice," he said with a smile.

"You're the second person to say that to me," Bev said.

"Well, it's a special year, you know. Full moon *on* the solstice. The energy's going to be off." He picked up his suitcase. "Best to hunker down to get through it. There's a lot of chaos to be had in this time. People acting strangely, you know how it goes."

Bev certainly did know, and she was getting a hunch that when Kemp said *chaos* and *energy* what he meant was *magic*. Could the solstice be causing the magical river that ran under Pigsend to act up? And was all that *chaos* connected to Zed's horses?

"Not my business," Bev muttered to herself.

Still, the caterpillar incident stuck in her mind, and she couldn't quite shake her curiosity. Of course, she might be able to take such a question to Percival, the wizard who lived in Lower Pigsend, but she wasn't keen on traveling there with the soldiers around. Someone closer to home might know the answer, though, and also would be pleased to know there were three loaves of bread baking in the oven for her.

Etheldra's tea shop was a short walk on the other side of town. It was a tidy little building with large front windows that looked onto a small seating room. During the summer months, Bev rarely saw anyone stopping to drink tea there during the day. Even now, the place seemed empty, except for the lone woman standing out front with her head in her hands. Shasta Brewer, one of the twins who worked there, still wore her apron as she openly sobbed.

"Shasta, dear," Bev said, hurrying over. "Are you all right? What's happened?"

"E-E-Etheldra j-just f-fired m-me," she stammered, her cheeks red and tear-stained. "Sh-she l-lost her m-marbles this morning over the t-tea being p-put in the wr-wrong spot."

"Oh, dear," Bev said, placing a comforting hand on her shoulder. "I'm sure it was all just a misunderstanding."

"N-no, sh-she told me to l-leave and n-never return." She wiped her eyes, but more tears fell. "I-I d-didn't m-mean to, but I-I d-don't know w-where m-my head is today. There are t-too many th-thoughts. I c-can't c-concentrate."

She stopped abruptly, as if someone had called her name. Not five seconds later, her sister Stella turned the corner and rushed to her side.

"Erm, Stella, it seems—" Bev began, but the twins seemed to be having a wordless conversation, staring deep into each other's eyes. Without a word, Stella put her arm around her sister and escorted her away.

"You take care of her," Bev said.

Stella jumped and blinked, as if she hadn't even noticed Bev was there. "Oh, goodness. How long have you been standing there?"

Bev chuckled. "Go on, you two. I'll talk with Etheldra. Go home and have some tea—"

Shasta's face screwed up into a sob.

"Er—something warm and comforting," Bev said with a nervous smile. "I'll try to put all this right."

She continued into the shop then stopped short. Bev had never been afraid of Etheldra per se, but the energy in the tea shop was definitely tenser than Bev had ever felt before. Etheldra stood behind the counter, ripping the tops off the tea tins and sniffing them before angrily shoving them on the counter. When the bell above the door tinkled, she stopped only for a moment to glare at Bev before turning back to her mission.

"What d'ya want?"

"Erm, Shasta left—"

"Good-for-nothing girl," Etheldra snarled. "Can't imagine how one person can mess up a shop so badly. Everything's in the wrong spot. The thyme next to the marjoram. Can you imagine such a thing? Dandelion next to the rose hips."

"Oh, what could be wrong with tins being next to one another," Bev said with a laugh.

"*Everything!*" Etheldra whirled on Bev, pointing a finger at her. "And you, standing there as you are. Bringing in the scent of rosemary on you."

"Now you're talking nonsense, Etheldra," Bev said.

"You're talking nonsense."

"Why in the world would you fire Shasta?" Bev asked. "She's been a faithful assistant for ages now, and things were well taken care of while you were gone."

"Harrumph!" Etheldra shook her head—almost too roughly, as if something were bothering her. "What is that incessant *buzzing*? Is it you? What with your stance like that. Straighten up. Who raised you?" She rubbed her face again. "And *what is that noise?*"

The energy is off, her guest Kemp had said earlier. Was that energy—or magic—causing Etheldra to act out this way? And if so, what did the solstice have to do with it?

"Etheldra, maybe you should close up shop and go home," Bev said. "I've got bread in the oven."

"Bread, who cares about bread? This whole shop is a mess. All the flowers are wrong."

Bev took a hesitant step forward. "Etheldra, I'm worried about you. You're acting erratic."

"If you've nothing valuable to tell me, you should leave," Etheldra snapped. "Be gone like that useless girl."

Bev took a hesitant step back then turned to leave. "I'm going to talk with Earl. Maybe he can get through to you."

~

The problem with finding Earl was the carpenter was never in one spot. Bev checked his workshop, his home, Etheldra's home, and everywhere else between. She asked Gore the blacksmith if he'd seen him (he hadn't), then found Jane Medlem the mason, who hadn't seen him either. She needed to get back to the inn, but her concern for Etheldra was more pressing. Surely, Earl could shed some light on her strange behavior.

Bev crossed the town square, still empty of the dragon fountain that Ramone, the local sculptor, had remade (or was remaking? Bev wasn't sure where that stood these days). The last she'd heard from them, they'd been put off reinstalling the fountain to make way for the wedding, which had been held here in the square. Perhaps the warmer temperature had soured them on the effort of installing it.

Or, more likely, they'd been stopped because there would be a display of fireworks on the night of the solstice. Bev snapped her fingers. That *might* be where Earl was. He was usually in charge of the event, and with the solstice only days away, he'd probably gone to Middleburg to get the fireworks.

To be sure, she headed toward the large building on the other edge of the town square. The town hall was an open space where town meetings were held. There hadn't actually been one since earlier in the spring, and for that, Bev was grateful. They were long, monotonous, and prone to tangents. In fact, the last event that had been held here was Etheldra and Earl's wedding.

Then, Vicky had decorated it with garlands and bundles of beautiful flowers, and it had been warm, inviting, and filled with love. Now, as Bev opened the front doors, the cavernous room was eerily quiet, and the squeaking of the floorboards was almost *too* loud.

There were two offices on either side of the meeting space. One, which belonged to Sheriff Rustin, was dark. Bev cursed her luck there; she was hoping the good sheriff might've seen Earl around. The other belonged to Mayor Jo Hendry, and her light was on.

The mayor sat at her desk, her brow furrowed in concentration as she read through papers. Her pale skin seemed shinier than usual, and her perfectly red lips were pressed into a thin line. The papers she read bore the queen's stamp, so perhaps that was the reason for her agitation.

"Yes, Bev, what can I do for you?" the mayor snapped, not looking up from the papers.

"I'm looking for Earl," Bev said.

"And you came to ask me?" She scoffed. "Despite what you might think, my duties as mayor don't include keeping track of every Pigsend citizen."

"I thought you might've sent him to Middleburg to get fireworks," Bev said, a bit put out that Hendry was being so rude. "But—"

"Right. I did." She softened. "Sorry. Not sure when he'll be back, though. I know he went today." With a groan, she rubbed her head before picking up the paper again.

"Are you all right?" Bev asked. "Distressing news from Queen's Capital?"

"No more than the usual fare," she said, sitting back. "I hear we have a cohort of soldiers staying to the north of us. Zed Mackey seems to have returned."

"Yes, and encountered a bit of trouble," Bev said, telling the mayor briefly about what had happened earlier that day.

"That's certainly a new one," Hendry muttered. "And he thinks Vellora's old commander is behind it?"

"He couldn't find any evidence," Bev said. "And I told him he couldn't arrest Andres without evidence, or else I'd…" She cleared her throat. "I'd go to Rustin."

Hendry barked a laugh. "You do know—"

"Yes, I'm quite sure Zed outranks him," Bev said. "But it seemed to appeal to his better instincts, as he let Andres go. In any case, I wanted to talk with Etheldra about what might've caused such a thing, but when I went to her shop, Shasta Brewer was outside crying. Etheldra fired her."

"Goodness," Hendry said without much enthusiasm.

"But more importantly, Etheldra was inside, tearing up her shop. Talking strangely about the tins being wrong and the plants acting strange. Even told me I was messing things up by standing there."

"Mm. Well, it was bound to happen sooner or later."

"That's it, though," Bev said. "She was acting like something was bothering her. Kept going on about a buzzing noise that was driving her batty."

At that, Hendry's dark eyes shot up to meet Bev's. "Really?"

"Yes. I think the buzzing is—"

"*I've* been hearing a buzzing for the past day,

too," Hendry said. "I thought it was just… Well, I don't know what I thought it was. But it's incessant. I was actually about to go home and down a bottle of wine to dull it." She tapped her finger to her chin. "Interesting."

"Do you think it has anything to do with the solstice?" Bev asked.

"Why would it have anything to do with that?" Hendry asked with a frown.

"Something a couple of my guests said to me," Bev said. "Something about it being a full moon at the same time. The *energy* is off. Maybe something to do with the magical river? Tides go up and down with the moon. Maybe magical ones do, too."

"That's a plausible theory," Hendry said, rubbing her temple.

Bev tutted. "Do you recall the last time there was a solstice around the full moon? I can't remember anything strange last year or the year before."

Hendry shook her head then seemed to regret it. "No, but my head isn't quite right today. I'm sure if you asked Max, he'd probably be able to find the answer for you." She groaned and rubbed her temples. "And if you find out, will you let me know? This is ghastly."

Bev had never seen the mayor anything but well put-together, so her head really must be hurting. "Do you need me to walk you home?"

"I'll manage," Hendry said with a thin smile. "Need to answer these letters before the post passes through tomorrow, otherwise, the responses will be late. And we're already in a bit of trouble as it is—"

"In what way?" Bev asked.

"Never you mind." Hendry winced as she rose. "You go on and chat with Max about this latest *curiosity*. I've got a date with a large bottle of wine."

Chapter Seven

Max came to dinner regularly, but it had been a while since Bev had visited him at the library. While the Pigsend branch held a tidy collection of books, Max's primary job was to keep meticulous records of everything that happened in town, from births, deaths, and marriages to the harvest totals to the *curiosities*, as Hendry had called them. Bev was sure, by now, she had a whole section in Max's archives, between the sinkholes and the Harvest Festival and the rest of it.

As she crossed the town square to the library, she pondered once again the six summer solstices she'd passed in Pigsend. The first, obviously, she didn't recall all that well. But the subsequent ones didn't merit mentioning, save the warm temperatures and evening celebrations. She hoped Max would be able to give her a straight answer about things, and that he wasn't afflicted by the same noise as Hendry and Etheldra.

"Ah, Bev!" Max seemed his normal self as Bev walked into the crowded library.

Most of the space was taken up by the scrolls and books containing the town records, but he had a few fiction and nonfiction titles. In his office, he had a box of so-called illegal books about magic and magical creatures, but Bev wasn't looking to peruse that today.

At least, she hoped not.

"Afternoon, Max," Bev said. "You'll be pleased to know there's rosemary bread in the oven right now. Should be getting back to it, but I wanted to ask you a question." She leaned on the counter. "I doubt you'd know this off the top of your head, but how common is it for the solstice to occur during the full moon?"

"Oh, it's not common at all," he said, brightening with excitement. "Great minds think alike, it seems. I was asking myself the same question last week when I realized we'd have a coincidence like that." He adjusted his glasses and walked to a stack of books, plucking one off the top. "The last one was perhaps fifty years ago."

"Really," Bev said with a look. "Was there

anything strange about that year?"

"Strange? In what way?"

"More produce, maybe a mention of magic?" Before the war, historians had a bit more leeway to talk about those things. "There's some weird stuff happening in town, and I'm wondering if the solstice has anything to do with it."

"Unfortunately, the historian during that time was, erm…" He cleared his throat. "Perhaps not as *detailed* as I am. An accounting of the moons, weather, and one brief mention of a surplus of produce. But other than that, nothing."

Bev deflated. "I see. Not very helpful."

"Not at all. I suppose one might ask the folks who were around fifty years ago, but they're probably few and far between," Max said. "I, myself, was studying at the great library during that time. Don't remember anything being amiss there, but it was so long ago." He tilted his head at Bev. "Why are you interested?"

"Just something a guest said to me," Bev said. "About the energy being off. And I came from Etheldra's tea shop. She's…erm…in a bit of a mood."

"Isn't she always?"

"More so than usual." Bev chuckled. "Biscuit's been acting strangely, too." She didn't want to mention Hendry, as it wasn't common knowledge that the mayor had magic. "The farms are overflowing with produce. My herb garden is growing like crazy." She ticked off her fingers. "And the soldiers up north—their horses got turned into caterpillars last night."

Max's eyes bulged. "I'm sorry, *what?*"

Bev told him briefly what had happened, and he laughed so hard his eyes watered.

"I shouldn't be so glib at others' misfortunes," he said. "But that's... Well, I don't want to say it serves them right, but it probably does." He wiped his eyes with his handkerchief. "Still, horses changing to caterpillars...that doesn't fit with the rest of it."

"How so?" Bev asked.

"Well, Etheldra's got a bit of magic about her. Your dog, Biscuit, I believe he's a laelaps, right?" Bev nodded, though she'd never told him that. "The produce, too, comes from that magical river that's underground. It runs right under the inn, so your herb garden." He also ticked off his fingers. "But horses turning into caterpillars...that's not a byproduct of magic nearby. That's someone using magic with *intent*. Someone wanted to cause trouble for those soldiers."

"Who has that kind of magic?" Bev asked. The only people she knew nearby who could've done that were the Lower Pigsend set, and they'd never risk bringing the attention of the queen's people to their little enclave.

"No idea," Max said. "Seems like there's another mystery afoot, isn't there?"

Bev wasn't excited by the idea, but she'd already suspected she was going to get roped into investigating one way or another. "It certainly seems that way. Zed thinks Vellora's commander's the one causing problems. They've got some bad blood in their history, and I'm sure it's coloring their expectations of each other. I'd like to find the real culprit before Zed decides to arrest him."

"Do you think it was a one-off?" Max asked.

"These things never are," Bev said wearily. "But I have a feeling if something else happens, Zed's going to detain Andres."

"Perhaps he should," Max said. "Then when the next thing happens, Andres will clearly not be responsible."

Bev chuckled. Somehow, she got the feeling Zed would find an excuse to keep him. "Will you be coming to dinner tonight? We're going to be having some lamb shank with cherry sauce."

Max clapped. "That sounds delicious! I do think I'll be joining you. I had a lovely walk and chat with Feliciano and Stephen yesterday evening. They're quite learned folks, you know." He smiled. "Not that it's not wonderful to live in Pigsend, but usually my only company for philosophical discussions is Bardoff, and his politics are quite different from mine."

Interesting. "Well, I'll be sure to save some for you, then. And if you find anything else about the solstice fifty years ago, let me know. Goodness knows, it would be nice to give these folks some answers."

"Indeed." Max made a face. "Let's hope the presence of rosemary bread is enough to improve Etheldra's mood."

~

All the rosemary bread in the world wouldn't help Etheldra, but Bev certainly had plenty to ponder as she worked on dinner.

Intent. Max had spoken about intentions, and as nefarious as some of the queen's people could be, she doubted Zed would transform his own horses into caterpillars just to find cause to arrest Andres. If that were the case, he would've just kept Vellora's commander under arrest instead of letting him go when he couldn't find evidence.

But that didn't mean Zed was completely innocent either. When Karolina Hunter had been in town, she'd put a contraption in the ground near Alice's farm. Their reasoning was if all the magic in town stopped, they'd have an easier time sniffing out the powerful person they were looking for. Could Zed have done the opposite? Flushing the town with magic so everyone with a hint of it would be easier to spot?

Bev didn't think so. She'd been through enough

of these "mysteries" to know that the culprits were most often found at her very own inn. After all, she had several people staying longer than one night. Andres wasn't completely out of the mix, even though he clearly had nothing to do with today's incident. Feliciano and Stephen, who'd gotten on so well with the illegal-magic-book-hiding librarian. Solan, the curious guest who'd told Bev to watch out for chaos during the solstice. Even Kemp was suspicious, though his arrival didn't quite fit the timeline.

Lots of theories, few answers, but it was so hot Bev could barely think straight. She had to take several breaks while making dinner to cool off. Biscuit, too, was agitated, walking around and sniffing the floor as if there was something delicious under the floorboards. Bev took pity on him and let him eat a few extra potato skins.

"You poor thing," Bev muttered. "Is your head too full of thoughts, too?"

He unfurled his tongue and panted at her.

"Well, I'm looking into it," Bev said, scratching him on the rear.

Feliciano and Stephen walked in, red-cheeked and sweaty from the day. Their hands were covered in dirt, and their boots were filthy.

"You two certainly look like you've been around," Bev said with a cheerful smile. "What did you get into today? I didn't see you much around the inn."

"Well, I daresay you were otherwise disposed," Feliciano said with a furtive look. "I saw you leaving with those soldiers this morning looking quite harried. Is everything all right?"

"Fine," Bev said. "A bit of a misunderstanding with Andres. The strangest thing happened, though. The soldiers' horses were somehow turned into caterpillars."

She scrutinized them, looking for signs of guilt or surprise or anything that might betray a hidden agenda. But stunned silence met her proclamation. Neither man looked like they'd expected her statement, let alone knew the cause of it.

"Did you say…caterpillars?" Feliciano said after a long pause.

"I did. Do either of you have any clue how that might've happened?" Bev asked.

They shared a look of confusion, and Stephen shook his head. "I don't think I've ever heard of such a thing. At least not since the queen took over."

"Even before. That's some advanced magic," Feliciano said then quickly added, "as I understand magic to be. I don't *practice* magic, of course." He chuckled nervously. "But in my travels, before the war, we spoke often with people with different abilities. To change the shape of a thing—"

"And not *anything*, but a living thing, too!" Stephen added. "Suppose the horses were all right when they turned back to normal?"

Bev nodded. "The soldiers were pretty irked, though. Eager to find out who might've been behind it."

"It wasn't us, if that's what you're asking," Stephen said with a look.

"No, just trying to get to the bottom of it," she said, hoping to diffuse their annoyance with a self-deprecating smile. "I don't know anything about magic, but Max tells me you two are learned men. I was hoping you might tell me more about it."

"We're learned, but not in magical things," Stephen said, almost too forcefully. "In any case, it *has* been a long day. Is there a place we can wash up for dinner?"

"Out back," Bev said, thumbing toward the kitchen. "Help yourselves. Should be some soap in the wash basin, too, if you need it."

They thanked her and headed quickly out the front room. Bev wasn't sure what to think of their conversation, except that there was definitely something they weren't telling her. Although Pigsend was a farming town, guests didn't usually show up covered in dirt.

"Another thing to think about, eh, Biscuit?" Bev muttered.

~

At six on the nose, Bev served dinner, but she couldn't help but notice Earl and Etheldra weren't in line with Max and the rest of the diners (including a couple of overnighters). Max said he hadn't seen either of them, nor had Bardoff.

"I'll pop by on my way home," Max assured her. "I'm sure everything's fine. They're not as young as they used to be. The journey back home probably wore on them."

Bev would've argued, except at that moment, Zed and the third of his soldiers walked in, surveying the room. Stephen sucked in a nervous breath, but no one else seemed overly unnerved. Kemp, the new guest, was too busy devouring his food, and Solan was humming to themselves and staring at the ceiling. If Max was bothered, he didn't show it.

"Erm, welcome back, Zed," Bev said, gesturing to the table. "Plenty of food for you and your fellow soldier tonight. And bread, too!"

"Where's Andres?" he said as he walked up to her.

"Is he under arrest?" Bev asked lightly. "Has something else happened?"

"No, but—"

"He left with Vellora," Bev said. "There was more meat to deliver. He told me not to expect him until sundown. Perhaps wanting to keep his head low while he's here." She smiled brightly. "Not that there's anything he needs to worry about, right?"

"Sure," Zed said after a long pause. His gaze

swept across the inn several times.

"You're here for dinner, right?" Bev prompted. "Take a plate."

She half-expected him to decline and sit in the corner to glare at everything that moved, but he took a plate and served himself. His soldier, who looked a little more approachable, introduced herself softly as Jemma while filling her plate.

"What is this?" she asked softly.

"Lamb with a cherry sauce," Bev said. "Mashed potatoes. Rosemary bread."

"That's what I'm smelling," she said with a nod as she took a slice. "It looks amazing."

"It won second place at the Pigsend Harvest Festival," Bev said, nodding to the ribbon above the fireplace. "Will you need food to take back to your fellow soldiers?"

"No, they've got plenty of supplies," she said, before casting her boss a nervous look. "Erm. I mean, they're getting more in. Um. That is…. We're fine."

Bev nodded. Clearly, Zed wasn't just here for a meal. "So, did you discover who turned your horses to caterpillars?"

"Not yet," she said, squirming a bit under Bev's questioning. She was young enough that she perhaps didn't know she could decline to answer. "But Commander Mackey says we're close."

"I'm sure you'll figure it out in no time," Bev

said. "Could be a quirk of the solstice. I hear there's lots of erratic behavior, what with the full moon and all."

Another thin smile, then she excused herself and hurried over to join her boss. Zed leaned over and asked her something and her pale cheeks went pink as she responded. He shook his head, shot Bev a sideways look, then dug into his meal.

Bev held her breath, waiting for them to do or say something, but they mostly kept to themselves. The other diners, however, seemed to finish their meals quickly and excused themselves. Bev couldn't help but notice that Max and the two guests didn't go out for another walk, perhaps unnerved by the soldiers. When it was Bev, Zed, and his subordinate in the room, Bev felt compelled to speak.

"I can't quite believe you came all this way to eat," she said. "Were you looking for something? Or someone, in this case?"

Zed rose with his empty plate, and almost mechanically, Jemma did as well, even though her plate was half uneaten. He crossed the room and handed it to Bev.

"Have you noticed anything else unusual lately?" he asked.

"Define unusual," Bev said. "As you'll recall, there was a curse on a wedding not too long ago."

"You know what I mean." His tone wasn't unfriendly, but it was firm.

"A few things, here and there." Bev gestured toward the table. "The farmers are practically begging me to take produce off their hands."

"I'm not worried about some extra produce," Zed said, waving her off. "But you're the one with an ear to the ground around here. If you hear of anything out of the ordinary—people acting strangely, assembling in odd groups, going off on their own." He nodded to her solemnly. "I want you to tell me, okay?"

Bev thought of Max and her guests, and their aligned politics, and of Hendry and Etheldra. "I'll try."

"It's important, Bev," he said. "You may not remember what it was like before the war, but we don't want to return to that time. And there are people out there who'll stop at nothing to reopen wounds better left alone." His gaze narrowed. "I have a feeling targeting our horses was an opening salvo."

Chapter Eight

Bev certainly *wasn't* going to tell Zed anything. But she did decide, as soon as he left, that she needed some real answers—and the only way she was going to get them was to visit Percival. She only hoped the wizard wasn't affected by the river, too.

A pair of guests had come just after the sun set late the night before and left as it came up, so Bev set to washing their sheets in the early morning sun. The backyard was still shaded, but by the time she returned from Lower Pigsend, they'd be dry and ready to be put away. She was nervous about making the trek, but the information she needed was important enough to risk it.

At seven, the front door opened, and Allen

walked in with a bright smile and a basket of muffins Bev could smell across the room.

"More blueberry, because Alice Estrich insisted," he said. "I hope you don't mind."

"You know I love everything you bake," Bev said, taking a particularly delicious-looking one and chowing down. But she only got one bite before her brows narrowed in suspicion. Once again, the taste was *too* good. Too perfectly blueberry, too fragrantly cinnamon. Biscuit's frantic tail wagging and sniffing nose at her side confirmed it.

"Allen, you've given me magical muffins again," Bev said with a sigh as she put down the half-eaten muffin.

"No, I haven't. I baked these." He picked one up and sniffed it. "I swear. Lillie wasn't even *in* the bakery yesterday."

"What's wrong with Lillie?"

"She's been complaining of a headache for the past three days, making silly mistakes, adding magic where she shouldn't have," he said. "I think half the pies I've been delivering have been laced with it, which explains why they keep doubling their orders."

"I don't think it's her fault," Bev said. She told him about the others, and the more she told him, the deeper his frown became. "Everyone I know who has a little magic is affected." She glanced up the stairs. "I'm headed to visit Merv to ask around.

I'd like to know what I'm dealing with."

Allen nodded. "Good idea. Especially with Zed in town. I saw him rampaging yesterday. What's going on there?"

Bev told him about the incident with the horses, and he predictably couldn't believe it. "Do you think it's connected with everyone having magic suddenly?"

"I don't know," Bev said. "There hasn't been a full moon coinciding with a summer solstice in about fifty years, but there might've been something funny going on then, too. I'm not so sure they're connected, either. The soldiers were targeted with intent, whereas everyone else seems to be a victim of some increased magic."

"Targeted? Who'd want to target my father?" He stopped, thinking about it. "Vellora, probably."

"And her commander, Andres. Your father is convinced he's in town to start a rebellion against the queen. He asked me last night to keep an eye out."

Allen made a face. "You aren't going to tell him anything, are you?"

"Of course not. At least, not without figuring out what's going on." Bev crossed her arms. "I was hoping to avoid a trip to see Merv while your father's around, but I don't think I can. I need some answers, and I don't know anyone else who might know." She tilted her head. "Maybe I can bring him these muffins. I'm not sure it's safe to serve them at the inn. I have a feeling your father's going to be a frequent visitor."

"Good point," Allen said. "Suppose I should head over to Sonny's, then. If Etheldra's on a tear, she's going to be furious if her morning scones are delayed."

"Yes, better to keep her tantrums to a minimum," Bev said.

"Hey, Bev, d'ya think…" He swallowed, looking almost a little hopeful. "Maybe my pobyd blood's woken up?"

Allen's mother had also been gifted with pobyd magic, though a very faint kind. Allen had gone so far as to bargain with a barus, a creature who could procure and give magic, to get some for himself (until Bev had intervened, of course). Bev had thought he'd put that dream to rest, but based on the expression on his face, perhaps not.

"Do you feel like it has?" Bev asked.

"I certainly don't feel any different." After a moment, he shook his head. "It's probably just Lillie's magic leftovers. I'll run over to Sonny's and get some fresh flour, just to be on the safe side." He sighed, flexing his hands again. "Wouldn't it be neat if I finally got my mother's magic, though?"

Bev smiled, almost hopeful that was the case. "You're a good baker without it, though. Look at what you've accomplished in the months since you started really trying."

"Yeah, and look at how much business has boomed since Lillie showed up," he said with a hearty laugh. "Still, I'm not sure she'll be around forever. So it would be nice if I could carry on with things myself."

"Just be careful who you serve a magical cookie to."

~

Bev hung around until all her remaining guests came down for the day to ensure she could apologize in person for the lack of breakfast pastries. She made up an excuse that Allen was positively swamped with orders and couldn't get to them. Everyone was understanding, of course, then went on their merry way. Andres went next door to the butcher shop, saying he was going to accompany Vellora on her meat deliveries. Stephen and Feliciano left without saying where they were going or when they'd be back. Solan retreated upstairs, complaining about the moon. And Kemp sat on the chair next to the hearth, a book in hand.

"Seems like a good day to stay in and read," he said. "What are you up to?"

"I've got to run an errand out of town," Bev said.

"What kind of errand?"

"Erm." She hadn't expected him to press. "Visiting an ill friend."

"Oh, well, I hope they feel better." He smiled. "When will you be back?"

"Hard to say. Hopefully before noon. The bread should be ready for the oven by then."

His face lit up. "More bread? Fantastic. That was the best loaf I've had in my life yesterday. And that's saying something. Last month, I was down in Rebashtown, where they really know how to make bread. Have you been there before?"

"Can't say I have," Bev said, inching toward the door. "But I do have to get on, so if you'll excuse me."

Once outside, she immediately scanned the street for any sign of Zed or his soldiers. She walked briskly through the town, keeping her head on a swivel as she took stock of every person on the street. She didn't relax until she was on the dirt path heading toward the farmlands, feeling confident, at least, that no one had followed her.

"I was wondering when you'd come see me again," Merv said as he opened the door to his small underground home. "What with all this magic floating around. I'm sure it's been hard for you, too."

"Oh, no." Bev frowned. "I was hoping it had spared you."

"I'm sure it's not quite as potent as it must be over in Pigsend, but I can tell it's here," he said, gesturing for her to come in. "I'm steeping a batch of iced tea, trying to cool down from this oppressive heat. But I'm sure Percival will be along in a moment."

Percival had cast an enchantment on Merv's living room to alert him whenever someone arrived —a handy thing, as the journey to Lower Pigsend would tack half an hour onto Bev's day. Instead, she could sit and enjoy Merv's tea while they waited for the wizard to make his appearance.

"Pardon, did you say iced tea?" Bev frowned. "Wherever did you get ice at this time of..." She paused. "Ah, never mind."

"There's a lovely young woman down there with the power to command the frost," he said, waddling out of the kitchen with a pitcher and cups on a tray. "She's making a tidy income right now. The line to get enchanted ice from her is longer than the one to see Percival these days."

"I can imagine," Bev said.

He set the tray down on the table in front of her. "I don't have anything delicious. Lillie hasn't visited in a little while—"

"Oh, I brought muffins," Bev said, almost as an afterthought. "Allen made them, but we're not sure if he's somehow come into his magic or if Lillie's is so out of control."

"I can imagine she must be feeling quite awful," Merv said. "Did you say Allen's magic? Has he come into his?"

"I'm not sure. There's pobyd magic in these, but we don't know whose."

"I may be able to tell." He popped the morsel into his mouth and chewed thoughtfully. "Hm. Hard to say. Definitely pobyd magic for sure. Might need to test a few more to really know for sure."

"Eat as many as you like," Bev said with a knowing smile. "Allen's gone to the miller to get more flour, in case, but I can't say he'd be sad if he finally came into his magic."

"Is he enjoying married life?" Merv asked.

"Oh, I didn't tell you!" Bev quickly gave him the story, including how Zed had used a forgetting potion on the cursed bracelet, so it would "forget" it had magic. "I asked him if such a thing could be used on a person with magic."

"That was dangerous," Merv said.

"Well, I'm curious about my past," Bev said with a shake of her head. "He didn't offer anything of interest, but I thought I might ask Percival."

"Ask Percival what?" Percival, an older man with a long beard and purple robes, appeared with a *pop* in the living room. Bev was pleased that, while aged, he still looked healthy and bright-eyed, as that hadn't been the case the first time she'd met him. "Bev, dear, how are you?"

"Embroiled in another curious happening in Pigsend, of course," Bev said with a sigh.

"I thought you might be. The magical river is

practically overflowing."

Bev nodded. "Are you having problems, too?"

"Not as much as you, I'd wager," he said. "We're far enough removed from the river that the effects are mild. But I can sense the amount running under your town. It's…well, it's not normal."

She'd been afraid of that. "Even with a solstice and full moon?"

He nodded. "The magical river ebbs and flows like a river of water, dependent on the phases of the moon. It's also pulled by the solstices and the position of the sun. When you have a solstice that coincides with a full moon, the magic swells like a flood. But right now, it's two or three times higher than that."

Bev told them about the soldiers' horses turning to caterpillars, and to their credit, neither Percival nor Merv seemed to think it was as out of the ordinary as the folks in Pigsend. Percival did agree with Stephen's assessment that it was advanced magic.

"I'd wager it's someone using all the excess magic to their advantage. Not many creatures possess that ability to transform like that," he said. "My assistant Shamus couldn't even do it."

"But you could?" Bev asked.

He nodded. "But I'm not the one responsible."

"Do you think there could be another wizard in town?" Bev asked.

"It's possible, though a soldier like Zed Mackey would be able to tell," Percival said. "Wizards can't really hide their magic."

Bev narrowed her gaze. "Unless there was too much magic in the air. Then they could hide in plain sight, couldn't they?"

"Yes, that's true." Percival chuckled. "Not that I want to test that theory, but if there's as much magic as you say, it would be difficult to find a wizard in it. Or any magical creature."

"So that could be a motive." Bev nodded slowly. "But to do what, I haven't a clue. I doubt someone would go through all that trouble just to be able to walk down the street." Still, she had more to go on than she had before. "Thank you, Percival. Since Zed is back in town, you may want to tell Officer Nog to lie low for a few days."

"Ah, Officer Nog seems to be..." Percival cleared his throat. "But he's taken a leave of absence from his duties. I'm sure he'll be back to work soon."

Bev didn't like the goblin and didn't want to pry, especially as he and Percival had something of a strained relationship. "Is there anything I can do to help my friends who are suffering?"

Percival thought for a moment. "Perhaps a tincture of willow and iron. Iron to dampen the effects of the magic itself and willow to ease the head pains. Boil the two in water for at least an hour."

"What kind of iron?" Bev asked.

"A few nails would suffice. Though…" He rubbed his chin. "If that soldier's as keen as you say, he might be suspicious of you walking around with iron water."

"Oh, maybe you could make a dessert!" Merv said. "A delicious solstice pie, baked with iron and willow bark. Something like a strawberry rhubarb would mask the flavors effectively, wouldn't it?" He hummed with anticipation.

The wizard nodded. "I believe so, yes."

That would certainly be less conspicuous. "I'll have to see Rosie about her willow tree again, too." Whether she'd let her take a branch was another story. Bev did, however, have one more question for the wizard, one that she'd been sitting on for a few weeks now. "I also wanted to ask if you're familiar with forgetting potions."

He nodded. "Very useful. They can break practically any spell."

"If a wizard took a forgetting potion, do you think they could forget they had magic?"

He sat back, considering the question as if it were a philosophical one. "I *suppose*. I've never heard of such a thing, though. No wizard in their right mind would…" He paused, eyeing her. "Well, I suppose things might've been different after the collapse of the kingside. Magical creatures might've wanted to forget their magic to remain safe from the queen."

"Is there an antidote?" Bev asked.

"I'm sure there might be one out there," Percival said. "But it's beyond my knowledge."

The clock on the wall chimed. "I should be getting back, lest any other calamities happen." Bev rose with a smile. "Thank you, Percival. I don't know what I'd do without you."

"We're still grateful for what you did for us a few months ago, and for the amulet you gave me," Percival said with a warm smile. "I can only imagine what Lillie must be feeling. That much magic is enough to turn even a non-magical person's head."

"Allen says she's got a wicked headache," Bev said, before frowning. "The iron in the crumble won't hurt her, will it?"

"No. It'll ease the pain," Percival said. "Allow her to regain control so it's not spilling into her baked goods."

Bev nodded to the muffins and smiled at Merv. "Have you figured out if the flour was laced with Lillie's magic or Allen's?"

So far, the moleman had eaten four. "Mm, no. Still hard to tell. Need more experimenting."

"If you're keen to know…" Percival said, pulling his wand.

Bev hesitated. Allen had looked so hopeful when they'd spoken earlier, and he'd once been so desperate to have a hint of his mother's magic that he'd nearly bartered away his entire business.

"Will everything go back to normal after the solstice?" Bev asked. "Everyone with enhanced powers will lose them?"

Percival nodded. "They should, yes."

"Better to let sleeping dogs lie, then," Bev said. "Thanks again!"

Chapter Nine

The trip was a success, and Bev was glad she'd taken the small risk to speak with Percival. Having him so close had been a boon for the various curiosities in town, even more than befriending Merv, who'd previously been her go-to guide for magical quandaries.

As she wasn't eager to see Rosie quite yet, her first stop was Gore Dewey, the blacksmith, for some iron. She saw him enough around town to be friendly, though she wasn't in need of iron materials too often, save the shoes for Sin and various tools. The shop was blisteringly hot as she opened the front door, but his apprentice Gilda Climber was the only one hard at work, banging on white-hot metal. Gore was talking with Freddie Silver, a farmer who lived southeast of the inn. Their conversation was tense, and when Bev walked in, they immediately stopped speaking.

"Morning, Bev!" Gore said, turning to her. "What can I do for you today?"

"Need some nails," Bev said, still watching Freddie with interest.

"Got a construction project at the inn?" Freddie asked.

"Yeah," Bev said. "How are you, Freddie? Still enjoying the newlywed life? How's Hans?"

He nodded, glancing at Gore for a moment. "Hans is good. Busy season, you know. Lots of crops to harvest this time of year. Our wheat is growing well."

Bev didn't think the river flowed over to their side of town, but she'd also never checked. "It's been a banner year for produce, that's for sure. The western farmers are practically begging me to take their fruit off their hands."

"Yeah, yeah. Spoke with Herman Monday about it the other day," Freddie said.

"Are you having any..." Bev wasn't sure how to phrase it. "Well, anything strange happening out your way?"

Freddie and Gore both started. "What do you mean strange?"

"Well, there's a group of soldiers in town," Bev

said. "They hit a spot of trouble."

"It wasn't *me*," Freddie said, almost too emphatically. "I've been hard at work at my farm. No trouble to speak of here, Bev."

Based on his face, there *was* trouble afoot. "I know a few folks have been feeling poorly, too, so —"

"Nobody feeling poorly," Freddie said with a stiff nod. "Everyone's fine. Perfectly normal solstice." He turned to Gore, a little pink on his cheeks. "Well… I'll see you around."

"Yes, I'll be sure to deliver that scythe," Gore said, with a slightly mechanical wave.

"Right, scythe." Freddie nodded, then all but sprinted out of the shop.

Bev stared between Gore and the door. "What was that about?" Bev asked.

"Nothing." Gore didn't sound too thrilled. "Nothing at all. Gilda?" He called, loud enough that his apprentice could hear him over the banging. "Can you help Bev? I've got to…erm…get an axe for Freddie."

"Scythe," Bev said mildly.

"Right." He turned back to her. "Scythe. See you around, Bev."

He, too, scampered away, leaving Bev alone with Gilda, who pulled off her mask and wiped sweat from her brow. She shook her head as she approached the front counter, and smiled at Bev.

"What's that about?" Bev asked.

"Don't ask me." Gilda shrugged as she pulled off her equipment. "He's been acting squirrelly the past week or so. Won't say much to me about it, other than disappearing for long stretches of time and leaving me to handle everything myself."

"Suppose that's good, isn't it?" Bev asked. The last time they'd chatted, Gilda had said she was about ready to end her apprenticeship. "Is he thinking of retiring any time soon?"

"No, which is part of my frustration," Gilda said with a sigh. "He won't release me from my apprenticeship unless I have somewhere to go. And I'd *love* to look farther than Middleburg or Sheepsburg, but—"

"You'd want to leave Pigsend?" Bev asked.

Gilda made a face, looking around as if checking to make sure no one was in the shop to overhear her. "*Yes*. It's such a small town. I'd like to settle down and start my own family one day, and the only eligible bachelor is Bardoff Boyd, who..." She made a face. "Too scholarly for me. And too old!"

"Allen's single now," Bev said, though she was mostly joking. She doubted Allen would want to even *hear* the word marriage for a long time. "But I understand. I hope you can figure it all out soon. We'd miss you if you left. Gore would, I know."

"He's got plenty of time to take on another apprentice," Gilda said. "And besides that, if he didn't want me to leave, he should make me a full partner in things, you know?" She blew air between her lips. "Don't know what my folks would say if I got a job elsewhere."

"Right, how are your folks?" Bev asked. "And your sister. Haven't seen her much since the wedding."

"If she knows what's good for her," Gilda said, "she's picking peaches and earning her keep. Not gallivanting around with that Norris kid and Vicky's brother."

Bev started. She hadn't even considered what PJ Norris must be feeling. Was his amulet enough to dampen the effects of the magical river? She hadn't seen any dragons around town, but it wouldn't hurt to check on him, too.

Gilda, oblivious of PJ's true nature, continued complaining about the teenaged trio. "Goodness knows Grant's turned into a right miserable cur now that he's got all that money. Or I suppose he's *going* to get all that money. Last I heard from Valta, they hadn't sorted it out yet, so he's still living off the stipend he got from his aunt." She snorted. "In any case, what was it you wanted? Nails?"

Bev had almost completely forgotten about her reason for being there. "Yes. Nails. Or any small scraps of iron you aren't using."

Gilda turned her head in surprise. "For what? Aren't you building something?"

Bev cursed herself for saying too much. "Nails will be fine."

~

Bev wasn't sure how many was too many, so she purchased twenty and stuffed them into her pocket as she girded herself for the next stop of the day. The last time she'd been in search of willow trees, Vicky had told her only one person in town grew them—Rosie Kelooke. At the time, Bev had sworn it would be smarter to plant her own tree than brave the woman again, but she hadn't gotten around to it. Now, dread grew in the pit of her stomach as she walked up the lane of houses.

Rosie was a retired seamstress who hadn't taken well to her new station in life. She could've given Etheldra a run for her money in the taciturn department, but whereas Etheldra's bluntness hid a kind heart, the same couldn't necessarily be said for Rosie. She'd lorded over poor Apolinary, the current seamstress, during Vicky's wedding preparations and almost driven the younger woman to madness.

Not to mention…

Cluck.

Bev stood in front of Rosie's yard, the willow tree a mere twenty paces away behind a wooden fence. And a large contingent of chickens. They had puffs atop their heads, which looked even puffier than usual. The chickens looked *bigger* than usual too, with talons sharp enough to leave deeper marks than the scars Bev already bore on her legs. Bev didn't want to traipse into the garden without an invitation. The chickens seemed to listen to Rosie better than anyone else, though with all the extra magic floating around town, would that hold true?

"Rosie?" Bev called.

Immediately, every fowl eye was on her. Bev hadn't ever *seen* them jump the gate, but there was a first time for everything.

"Nice chickens," Bev said, holding out her hands. "I'll stay here, and you stay over there, and we'll call it even, okay?"

One with a particularly large pouf on his head strutted forward, his beak clacking menacingly.

"Just here to have a chat with your, erm… With Rosie. No need to get your feathers in a twist." Bev glanced at the door and called louder, "Rosie? Are you there?"

Finally, the front door swung open, and the old woman stepped out with narrowed eyes. "What do you want?" she snapped.

Great. "Good morning, Rosie. I was wondering if I might borrow some of your willow bark again."

She let out a snort. "Why in the world would I let you have that?"

"Because it's the neighborly thing to do?" Bev said with a sideways glance. "Just a bit of it. Your tree's so large, I'm sure you can spare it." She swallowed, remembering their last deal. "Be happy to bring you a loaf of bread as payment."

She considered it for a moment. "Yes, that sounds fine."

"Right, I'll—"

"And while you're at it," Rosie continued, sounding a bit less firm, "go to the farmers' market and bring me a crate of fruit and vegetables, too."

Bev started. That was certainly an odd request. Rosie wasn't infirm in the least, and could handle the short trek to the west side of town.

"Sure thing," Bev said, eager to close the deal.

"And corn for the chickens," Rosie said, her face taking on an odd expression. "I think they're quite hungry, and I've run out."

Bev stopped, for the first time really examining Rosie. Her dress seemed like it hadn't been cleaned in some time, and the bottom hem was in tatters, as if it had been caught in a thorny bush. Her hair was askew. And she hadn't once left the safety of her front door.

"Rosie, are you trapped in your house?" Bev asked, tilting her head.

She barked a laugh. "How ridiculous, of course I'm not—"

The lead chicken, who'd been staring down Bev, turned and clucked ominously.

Rosie inched backward into her home, fear clear on her face as she laughed nervously. "Well, perhaps the chickens are a *bit* more ornery than usual. But they'll settle soon, I'm sure."

As if on cue, the chickens began squawking loudly, flapping their wings and landing on the front step of Rosie's house. She yelped and dashed inside, slamming the door behind her. A moment later, she opened her front window and peered out, keeping her gaze on the chickens before turning back to Bev.

"Well? What of it." She scowled. "So I'm trapped. Come to gloat?"

"Of course not," Bev said softly. "You poor dear. How long have you been stuck here?"

She swallowed, her pride finally defeated. "Three days. I'm nearly out of food. Can't pump water, either. It's a mess. I think if I had some corn, I'd be able to get past them while they were distracted, but I'm fresh out." She sniffed, shaking her head at the chickens. "I haven't a clue what's come over them."

Bev did. The magical river ran beneath Rosie's backyard, hence why a sinkhole had eaten her recently-constructed brick oven. Now, her chickens were presumably suffering from the same ailment as the rest of Pigsend. Whether the chickens were actually magical or ornery from the excess magic, Bev didn't know. In the past, Rosie had shown sympathies for the queen's people, so it would be odd if she had a flock of magical chickens. But stranger things had happened.

"The market's still open," Bev said. "Herman told me a few days ago he had a surplus of corn. I'll head there right now and pick some up." She placed her hand on the fence. The lead chicken opened its wings and flapped and Bev removed it quickly. "Erm. Do you think that'll do it?"

Rosie nodded. "I think so. At least long enough to get you to the willow tree."

"Oh, forget the willow," Bev said. "We have to get you out of your house. You can't possibly be trapped there until after the solstice."

Her eyes widened. "What do you mean, until after the solstice? What's happened to my chickens?"

"Just a bit of solstice madness," Bev said, hoping that explanation would suffice. "I'll go get the corn. You hang tight. We'll get this fixed, I promise."

~

Bev stopped at the inn only long enough to leave the nails—which were poking her in the leg whenever she walked—and check on her bread. The loaves weren't ready for the oven but would be by the time she got back, so she started the ovens and left Biscuit in charge.

The market, once again, was overflowing with produce, and Bev didn't have to go far to find what she was looking for. Herman Monday had several bags of corn ready to be cooked and was more than happy for Bev to take them off his hands.

"Bathilda's no longer buying from me," he said. "She was taking all the corn she could get her hands on last year, then suddenly, she stopped. Of course, now I have more than I know what to do with." He shook his head. "Become snippy, too, you know?"

"Alice said the same," Bev said, a little concerned about the farmer. Was she ill because of the magic, too? More people to deliver crumble to, it seemed.

"Maybe you should take another bag of corn, then. Or two. Maybe three!" Herman said with a little pleading in his voice.

"I'll have to come back for more," Bev said. "I didn't bring the wagon today." She scanned the rest of the farmstead, spotting a pile of rhubarb next to a small crate of strawberries. "I'll take those off your hands, though."

"Perfect for a solstice pie!" he said, looking overjoyed. "The lot of them? Making a delicious meal for the inn?"

"Something like that," Bev said, handing over payment. The farmers, at least, were making their money for the year. "Say, Herman. You've lived in town a long time, right?"

"My whole life!" he announced. "My great-grandaddy settled here and started the farm. Proud to carry on the tradition."

"Do you ever remember a solstice being so… strange? In terms of an overabundance of produce," Bev asked. "Maybe one when you were a boy?"

"I can remember one, yeah." He pushed his cap atop his head as he scratched his forehead. "Felt kinda like this. Produce was growing like mad, everyone was happy. If I remember right, we made enough that summer to go on holiday the following spring."

"Was it this...plentiful, though?" Bev said, gesturing to the bags and bags of corn sitting beside him.

"Maybe not this much, no. Whatever's going on seems to be once in a lifetime, you know?" He pointed to the rhubarb. "That rhubarb's been sitting in my root cellar for three weeks now. Strawberries, too! You'd think they'd have gone bad already. But no, still as plump and fresh as the day I picked 'em."

The magic certainly was doing its job. "Strange, indeed," Bev said.

"I can't say I mind it. You should see my pumpkins, Bev!" He grabbed his suspenders proudly. "They're bigger than last year's already! Going to take ten men to get them down to the Harvest Festival." He cracked a wry grin. "Ol' Trent won't know what hit him." He rubbed his hands together greedily. "He got lucky last year with that Harvest Festival mishap. But this year... This year is mine to win, Bev!"

Chapter Ten

The inn actually felt cool after being in the midday sun, but the oven was hot and ready for the bread. Bev tossed in the loaves and placed the produce on the kitchen table before sitting and resting a moment, wiping her brow and neck with a washcloth.

"Cooler weather can't come soon enough," she muttered.

But she thought of Rosie, and couldn't rest long. She husked the ears of corn so the chickens would be able to devour them quickly, then prepped the rhubarb and strawberries to be made into a crumble later. By the time all that was done, the bread was ready to be pulled from the oven.

"I'm sure we can spare one for poor Rosie," Bev said, wrapping one of the piping hot loaves in a tea towel and tucking it next to the root vegetables in her basket.

"You stay here, Biscuit," she said, putting the basket on one arm and hoisting the bag of shucked corn over her shoulder. "Don't want you getting tangled up with these chickens."

Biscuit promptly went to his spot by the hearth and fell asleep.

With a sigh, Bev headed out the door and back into the bright sunlight. The walk through town seemed longer than usual, and Bev thought more than once she should've brought a hat. But all her annoyance went out the window as she walked up to Rosie's house and thought about the poor old woman trapped by a flock of demonic chickens.

"We'll get you out, Rosie," Bev muttered, adjusting the bag on her shoulder. "And if not, Herman's got more corn."

Rosie stepped out of her front door the moment Bev walked up; clearly, the older woman had been waiting for Bev to return. She fiddled with her hands, looking nervous.

"I wasn't sure you'd come back," Rosie said. "I know we've—"

"I'm not going to leave you stranded here, Rosie." Though as she approached the fence, some of her confidence waned at the first *cluck*. She held her breath and pulled out the first ear of corn, holding tight to the basket of food. "All right. Let's see what this does."

She tossed the corn into the center of the the yard. Immediately, every one of the chickens squawked loudly and pounced on it. Bev flung open the gate and dashed into the yard. The chickens that hadn't gotten to the ear fast enough turned on her, opening their wings as if ready to attack, so Bev tossed another at them. They attacked that, but by now, the ones on the first ear had eaten every kernel, and turned their attention back to Bev.

She reached into her bag again, tossing two more ears on either side of her, splitting the difference between the two groups. And then, with a gasp, she flew onto Rosie's front porch. The other woman grabbed her by the arm and yanked her to safety.

After catching her breath, Bev straightened and smiled, thrusting the basket at Rosie. "Food. For you."

Rosie actually looked on the verge of tears. "Bev, I don't know what to say…"

"Thank you is all I need," Bev said. "Can't believe you've been here all this time. And no one came to…" Bev didn't want to hurt Rosie's feelings, so she didn't finish. "Well, we've got it sorted now. Plenty of corn left in the bag."

Rosie sank into the nearby rocking chair and

broke the still-hot bread in half. Bev winced, as she usually waited until the bread was completely cool before cutting into it, but Rosie started stuffing it into her mouth, so Bev let her eat.

"Oh, that hits the spot," Rosie said, sitting back.

"I know a place you could get rid of these monsters." Not that she wanted to unleash demonic chickens on Lower Pigsend, but at least there were magical creatures who could handle them better. "If you want."

Her face screwed up into tears. "Oh, I could *never!* These chickens, I've raised many of them from eggs. They're my babies. They're having a time right now, that's all." She turned to the front yard, where the chickens had devoured the corn, cobs and all. "But, erm, you did bring more corn, right?"

"I did." Bev raised the bag. "I'll leave you with some so you can get out. Herman Monday's got plenty, so I'm sure he'd be happy if you took it off his hands. But if you need help, please don't be too proud to ask for it. I have a feeling things won't calm down until after the solstice."

She nodded, wiping her eyes. "You're a true friend, Bev. Thank you for coming to help me. I'm so sorry I've been cross with you before."

Bev patted her shoulder. "I have a short memory, you know."

Rosie chuckled and wiped her eyes again. "Well, I think I can manage from here. You said Herman

Monday's the one selling corn?"

Bev nodded. "At the farmers' market on the west side of town. Probably still be there if you hurry."

Rosie smoothed her hair, making a face. "I'm not fit to be seen by anyone right now. I'll head out in the morning." She raised the basket in thanks. "Planning on eating well this evening. Thank you again."

"Happy to help. Now," Bev turned to the yard, and the willow tree ahead of her, "wish me luck. I've got a branch to steal."

~

It took three more ears of corn, most thrown by Rosie from the porch, for Bev to retrieve several branches from the willow tree and dash to safety. Bev didn't think she took a breath until she was clear of the fence. She waved her thanks to Rosie, who still had six ears of corn left to get herself out of her house. Still, Bev thought it a good idea to let Earl or someone else know about her predicament. No one, not even Rosie Kelooke, deserved to be trapped in their house by a flock of demonic chickens.

Willow branches in hand, Bev returned to the inn, finally ready to put her concoction together. She dug through the collection of recipe cards Wim McKee had left her when she'd inherited the inn and found his recipe for strawberry-rhubarb crumble. Wim didn't typically make desserts at the inn, a tradition Bev had followed, but he did have a few recipes stashed away for special occasions.

She read through the card, then retrieved the butter and sugar from her root cellar, grateful she didn't need to call on Allen for it. He might not even be there (though she'd let herself into the bakery before when he hadn't answered the door), and if he was, he'd be busy making pies. Not to mention…the nagging question of whose magic was lacing their products. Bev didn't have much of a liar's face. She was keeping Allen's powers a secret out of care for him, but she still wouldn't be able to fool him. Best to leave them alone for the moment.

Per Wim's recipe card, the solstice fruit crumble called for a few heaping handfuls of chopped fruit (*any kind, but it must be ripe and delicious*). To that, she would add sugar, a little flour to help coat it, and the juice of a lemon, if she had one, and a pinch of salt to really enhance the flavors. Then she would combine together flour, butter, and sugar and crumble it over the mixture for a delicious texture once baked.

She started by cutting the strawberries in her large bowl. Like every other piece of produce Bev had purchased, the berries were exquisite, and several of them barely fit the palm of her hand. As she cut into them, the scent of sweet juice was too much, and she had to sneak a bite. Flavor exploded in her mouth as if it were one of Lillie's magically-laced confections.

"Hopefully not too much magic in these berries," Bev muttered, popping another strawberry into her mouth. The rhubarb, too, was magnificently colored, and mixed together with the strawberries, they were a vision of green and red. Bev finished the filling recipe, using the last of the lemons she'd gotten from Allen.

Before she turned to the crumble topping, she thought to tackle the willow bark. She first tried her potato peeler, but found the wood too tough, so she opted for a small paring knife instead. As soon as she had enough shavings to fill the cheesecloth, she bundled it with a few nails, tied it off, and—

"What are you doing?" Kemp stood in the doorway.

Bev had been so engrossed in shaving the willow she hadn't even heard the door open. "Kemp, you gave me a fright. Can I help you with something?"

"I heard you down here and thought..." He walked into the kitchen, eyeing the shaved wood and cheesecloth. "What kind of wood is that?"

"Willow bark," Bev said. "It's going inside the crumble as an...aromatic."

"Willow bark?" He scoffed. "An aromatic? Maybe for a woodpecker."

Bev nestled the satchel into the rhubarb and strawberries and started working on the topping, hoping Kemp would get the hint and leave her be. "Can I help you with something?"

"Is that rhubarb and strawberry?" he asked, peering into the bowl. "Are you serving it for dinner?"

"No, I'm not," Bev said, resisting the urge to swat his hand away from her pan. "I mean, you're welcome to have some, but—"

"I have to say, I'm a bit curious what willow shavings add to this sort of pie," he said, picking up the satchel and sniffing it. "It doesn't *smell* like—"

Bev snatched it from him and replaced it in the pan. "As I said, you're welcome to try it later, if you like. But if you must know, there's a…summer cold making its way around town. It's too hot for tea, but willow bark is a good pain reliever. I'm letting it cook with the berries and rhubarb. It'll be a treat and a balm."

"Oh." That seemed to make sense to him. "Well, I'm so sorry to hear your friends are ill, but it seems silly to ruin a perfectly good crumble with the taste of willow, and…what else is in there? I felt something hard, and—"

"I've done this before," Bev said, though she clearly hadn't. She got a funny feeling about Kemp and wanted him out of her kitchen. As she busied herself with mixing the flour, sugar, and butter for the topping, she plastered on another fake smile. "Thank you so much for your advice, but I've got it."

"If you're sure—"

"Very." She beamed at him. "Dinner's at six! Looking forward to chatting more then."

"Sounds good." He turned to go—thank goodness—before he reached the door, he spun around. "Say, what do you know of the bakers next door?"

"The bakers?" Bev stopped. "Why?"

"Just curious. I've had a few of their muffins for breakfast now, and I think they're quite good. Almost too good, you know?" He smiled, as if that hadn't set off warning flags in Bev's mind. "Are they from this town?"

"Yes," Bev said, not wanting to divulge any more about Lillie than was necessary. "They're quite busy these days."

"I can tell. I keep trying to go over there and talk with them, but they're always closed for deliveries." He chuckled. "You'd think they'd be able to hire someone to make those for them if they're that busy, you know?"

"Well, if I see them at their post, I'll be sure to let you know," Bev said. "But in the meantime...I do have to get this in the oven."

Thankfully, Kemp *did* finally get the hint, or the heat in the kitchen was too much for him, because he left her soon after that. Bev wasn't sure exactly what it was about the man that put her on edge, or if it was merely because he was asking questions she didn't want to answer. But he seemed almost a little *too* curious about the comings and goings of Pigsend residents, and Bev didn't like him asking questions about Lillie and Allen.

"One crisis at a time," Bev said, returning her attention to the crumble. She finished adding the topping and placed it in the warm oven, saying a small prayer it would cook well. It wasn't long before the entire kitchen smelled of sweet strawberries and tart rhubarb, not to mention butter and sugar. Bev hoped the willow wouldn't be too difficult to get out, but the crumble topping was such that she could move some of it to the side, remove the willow bark and iron nail pouch, and move the browned sugary top to cover the gap. She even snuck a taste.

"Mm." She closed her eyes, marveling at her own handiwork. Merv had been right—the tartness from the rhubarb covered up any aftertaste. "That would be fit to serve from the bakery, I'd say."

She wanted to be sure, especially before walking all over town with the syrupy, scrumptious crumble, that it worked. And lucky for her, she had an afflicted magical creature currently walking holes in her front room. He barely acknowledged her as she approached, and it wasn't until she started scratching his rear that he stopped and looked at her.

"You all right?" Bev asked, moving to rub his ears. "I've got something I hope will help."

He unfurled his tongue in a happy smile then sniffed at the small portion in the bowl as she dumped it out on the ground. But, surprisingly, he didn't go for it like he did literally every other piece of food.

"Oh, come now," Bev said with pursed lips. "Eat that. I'll make you feel better."

He sniffed it again then sneezed, as if it smelled awful to him.

"Percival told me it would help," Bev said with a quiet whisper. "Now stop being ridiculous and take your medicine."

Finally, Biscuit lowered his head, his tongue darting out to taste it. He made a face, coughing. But after a moment, he sat, shaking his head. The tension that had kept his little body moving eased slowly, and he yawned.

"Better?" Bev asked.

He rose and walked to the hearth, circling for a moment before lying down and going to sleep immediately. Before long, his loud snores echoed through the room, a sound Bev realized she hadn't heard in several days. She smiled, walking over to scratch him on the head lovingly.

"I'll take that as a yes," she whispered. "You get some rest. You've certainly earned it. I've got to take this to the poor, afflicted residents of Pigsend."

Chapter Eleven

With a bowl of crumble in hand, Bev crossed the street to the butcher shop. She knocked on both the front and back doors, but no one answered. She hadn't seen Ida in a few days, and had to assume she was upstairs sick in bed, so she vowed to return later. Her next stop, the bakery, was also closed for the day, and Allen had presumably left to deliver all the custards and cakes he'd been working on.

"Tea shop it is."

It was even more of a mess than it had been before. The tins were all open, contents strewn all over the place. Etheldra didn't seem to notice or mind, muttering to herself as she dug her fingertips into the dried herbs and sniffed them.

"Be gone with you," she barked as Bev walked into the shop. "I don't want to hear from you or your rosemary."

"I've brought you something to make you feel better," Bev said, approaching nervously. She wasn't sure if Etheldra would take the crumble or toss it on the floor. "Might help with all the, erm, voices."

Etheldra eyed her for a long moment, and Bev finally noticed the faraway look in her gaze. "I don't know…"

"Just a bite. Let me know how it tastes." Bev put the bowl on the counter and stepped back, holding her breath.

Etheldra stepped forward and sniffed it, giving Bev a sideways look before spearing a strawberry and shoving it in her mouth. She chewed thoughtfully for a moment, and Bev feared the crumble might not be potent enough. But as she scooped up another mouthful, the tension began to leave her face, as it had Biscuit's.

"What did you put in this?" She shook her head then swayed.

"Steady on," Bev said, rushing forward to catch her and help her sit in a nearby chair. "Are you all right?"

"I feel…" She blinked heavily then an oddly relaxed smile spread across her face. "I feel so much better!" She turned to the bowl and scooped up more. "Whatever you put in this, it's working. Bit metallic for my liking, taste-wise. I wouldn't be serving this at the inn. But—"

"It was baked with iron," Bev said. "And a little satchel of willow bark to help ease some of the excess magic in your blood," Bev said, grateful to hear her old friend sounding more like herself. "You've been out of sorts the past few days."

"Has it been that long?" Etheldra surveyed her shop. "Did I do all this?"

Bev nodded. "Not exactly sure why, but—"

"I told you once I've always had a preternatural ability with herbs," Etheldra said, picking up one of the tins and sniffing it. "But since we returned, it's been as if…the plants could talk with me. And they had lots of opinions, I'll tell you that much. This one didn't want to be with that one, and that one didn't like the look of this one. Every time I stepped into the shop, the lot of them were arguing with one another. And even when I left, I could hear the grasses all the way home. Thirsty, ready for rain." She rubbed her temples. "Where's that Brewer girl? This is going to be a mess to clean."

"You fired her."

Etheldra's gaze snapped up. "I did *what?*"

"You said… Well, you weren't in your right mind," Bev said. "I'll be happy to find her, and—"

"No, no. Best I do it. Swallow my pride and all that." She scraped the remains of the crumble. "Now that I'm back in my right mind."

"Hopefully, it should get you through the solstice," Bev said.

"Solstice?" She narrowed her gaze. "What does that have to do with anything?"

Bev explained what she'd learned from Percival, and Etheldra nodded knowingly, especially when Bev mentioned the last time the two had coincided. "I remember that summer. I was a young girl, but I recall feeling…" She shook her head. "Well, not this bad, but a little flighty. This was something else entirely."

"Someone's definitely doing something to the river," Bev said.

"And what have you done about it?"

Bev gave her a look. "Nothing, yet. Too busy trying to keep my dear friends from losing their good senses."

She sighed, rising. "Well, I'd love to stick around and theorize with you, but I find myself ready to take the longest nap of my life. Been a few days since I've been able to really settle in, you know?"

"You go rest," Bev said, helping her to stand. "Then find Shasta."

"Yeah, yeah."

~

After a quick stop at the inn to get two more bowls, Bev headed north to Mayor Hendry's home and Wilda Murtagh's, where Lillie rented a room.

Hendry was, unsurprisingly, at home and looking quite disheveled. She turned her nose up at the gift until Bev told her its purpose, and she gratefully took the bowl. She took a single bite, blanched as if it were poison, thrust it back into Bev's hands, then slammed the door.

Bev, who was used to this sort of behavior from Hendry, simply shook her head and left.

Wilda lived three houses down from Hendry, in a tidy little cottage where she made and sold candles. Lillie had been renting a room there for the past month, since the wedding had all but evicted her from the Weary Dragon. But she'd indicated she was ready to put down some roots, so the timing was all fine for her. Wilda, too, was happy to have a baker living with her, especially as it meant an overabundance of unsold pastries.

To wit, after knocking, Bev let herself in and spotted an assortment of scones, pastries, and other confections on Wilda's kitchen table.

"Lillie?" Bev called. "Are you up there?"

"Somewhat," came a weak voice up the stairs. "Come on up."

Bev followed the sound and gently pushed open the door, immediately hit by the smell of cinnamon. Lillie was lying flat in a small bed, Merv's quilt visible beneath her, with a rag over her eyes. She waved sadly, and when she did, the small salted crackers by her fingers lifted upright and danced around each other.

She lifted the rag and groaned. "Oh, bother. Not again. Stop it. Stop it, you." She swatted at the crackers, and they fell flat on the table. "Bev, dear. I hope everything is all right. I'm so sorry I haven't been in the bakery. My head won't stop aching, and every time I even lift a finger, my magic infuses anything with flour in it. It's all I can do to keep it hidden from Wilda at breakfast."

"Poor thing." Bev sat next to her on the bed. "I've brought you something."

"Crumble?" Lillie sat up, sniffing it. "Oh, but you've baked it in something. It smells..." She inhaled deeply and made a face similar to Biscuit. "What's in that?"

"Medicine."

As with Biscuit, Lillie only needed a small taste before she felt the effect. She practically threw down the bowl and reached for the water, but after a moment, the tension between her brows eased. "Oh, yes, Bev. That did the trick. Nasty stuff, but—"

"Cooked with iron," Bev said.

"Yes, that's exactly what it is," Lillie said with a disgusted look. "It's bitter, you know? Like too much lemon."

Bev took another bite. It tasted fine to her. "Everyone with magic who's tasted it thought it was disgusting."

"Who else?" Lillie asked.

"Biscuit, Etheldra, Hendry," Bev said. "Going to take it to a couple more folks in town."

"Hendry?" Lillie said thoughtfully. "I didn't realize she had magic. I bet that's how she keeps getting reelected. Goodness knows I hear enough about her from Wilda. I bet she's spelling everyone to get her way."

"You're probably not wrong," Bev said. "I think there's another election this year. Maybe someone will finally get the better of her."

"If there's one thing I've learned about living here, it's that you never know what's going to happen next," Lillie said. "First Allen and Vicky's wedding gets cursed, now everyone in town's got magic. Have you figured out what's going on?"

"Percival says the magical river ebbs and flows with the moon, and it being a solstice full one means it's at its highest point." She sighed. "But he thinks, as I do, that it's even higher because someone's doing it."

At the mention of the wizard, Lillie's face softened and grew sad. "Oh, you went to see Merv? How is the dear moleman?"

"Wonderful. Happy to get some magic-laced muffins." Bev winked. "I take it you still haven't..."

"Well, I'd planned on it after the wedding, but then we got so busy with solstice orders, and..." She shook her head. "Still feeling a bit embarrassed about the whole thing, to be honest." Lillie tapped her fingers on the bowl. "In any case, I'm sure Allen's drowning without me there. Now that I'm feeling better, I should head over and help him out."

"Lillie," Bev said quietly. "I think Allen might have pobyd magic now."

"What?" Lillie shook her head. "Why do you say that?"

Bev told her about the muffins, and Merv confirming the magic in them. "Percival offered to determine their source, but I declined."

"Why?"

Bev looked out the window thoughtfully. "If Allen were to find out he had a bit of his mother's magic only to lose it when the river ebbs, it might break his heart. He's always been rather funny about it, you know? I thought it might be better to just keep it from him."

Lillie nodded. "That makes sense. He's such a good baker, though, even without the magic. He's got good instincts on flavor. And you know, it's entirely possible my magic just seeped into all our flour. Once I get back to the bakery, I can probably remove it."

"Probably a good idea, especially with Zed in town," Bev said.

"Don't mention him," Lillie said, squeezing her eyes shut. "I get a swooping feeling every time he walks by the bakery. Thankfully he hasn't come to call. I think he and Allen have gone back to pretending the other doesn't exist. Which suits me fine." She turned to Bev. "Is there anyone else in town who's got magic like me?"

"There is one, erm, person I know of," Bev said. "But I haven't seen any fire-breathing dragons."

"I'm sorry… *Fire-breathing dragon?*" Lillie's eyes nearly fell out of her head. "You didn't tell me about that!"

"Nothing to tell," Bev said, waving her off. "And I'm going to pop by just to make sure that remains the case."

Said fire-breathing dragon shifter, young PJ Norris, lived with his parents Pip and Holly near Earl's workshop. Bev peered around the fence to see if the carpenter had returned, but it was empty. Etheldra had said he was busy preparing for the solstice fireworks, but she still wanted to let him know his bride had been cured.

Bev walked up to the Norrises's front door and rapped a few times. Holly answered, worry clear on her face, and Bev was glad she'd made the trek.

"B-Bev. Hi. What can I do for you?"

"Just checking on PJ," Bev said. "Erm. Is he…?"

"Come in." Holly opened the door and all but yanked Bev inside.

There, she found PJ sitting in front of the fire, holding a bucket and looking ready to vomit. Next to him, a large mint plant had almost been picked clean. He looked up as Bev approached and waved weakly.

"How are you feeling?" Bev asked, kneeling in front of him.

"Awful." As he spoke, a puff of smoke wafted toward the ceiling. "My stomach's on fire."

"Rita said he wouldn't get like this again," Holly said, fretting at her hands. "What's going on?" Bev told her, and Holly let out a frustrated sigh. "Well, goodness. What next?"

"The good news is I have something that will hopefully help," Bev said. "If you need more, I have it at the inn. But hoping a little will do the trick."

"Is this…?" PJ lifted the spoon, suspiciously. "It looks half-eaten."

"Well, I can head back to the inn to get you a fresh bowl, or you can eat that and see if it makes you feel better," Bev said.

PJ shrugged and took a big bite. He looked like he was going to puke again, but Bev coaxed him to eat even if he didn't like the taste. He swallowed with some difficulty, and a moment later, the color returned to his face.

"That's better," he said with an exhale that contained a little smoke.

"As I said, there's more at the inn," Bev said to Holly. "Best to keep a low profile until the solstice passes anyway. Zed Mackey's back in town—"

"I saw him," Holly said, putting her hand on

PJ's shoulder. "You don't think he's in town to find the dragon shifter, do you?"

"He hasn't mentioned it, but he's a bit preoccupied," Bev said. "His horses turned into caterpillars."

PJ snorted, as if that were the funniest thing he'd ever heard, and his mother glared at him. "Pip Junior, I *know* you aren't so stupid as to—"

He shook his head firmly. "I swear, it's not me. Or Grant or Valta. We don't mess with queen's soldiers. In fact, we're trying to get *away* from them."

"What do you mean?" Bev asked.

PJ and Holly shared a look, and Holly's eyes filled with tears. "I'm moving to Sheepsburg," he said.

"You're moving?" Bev frowned at Holly. "Who'll shoe the horses?"

"Not me, just...PJ," Holly said. "It's a larger city. More...things happen there. PJ would better be able to hide from the queen's soldiers. My mother was happy to let him stay for a few weeks, and he seemed to really like being there." She teared up, looking at him.

A similar feeling welled in Bev's chest. "I'll miss you, PJ. When are you leaving?"

"In a few weeks," he said. "Gram's trying to get the three of us enrolled at university there, but don't tell Grant. I only got him to agree to come because he *wouldn't* have to live with his snooty aunt and listen to her rules. But Vicky seems to be enjoying herself, so it can't be all bad. And she'd be delighted to have Grant close by."

Bev smiled at him, his impending departure bittersweet. "Make sure you pop by the inn before you leave and give me a proper goodbye. It'll be strange to not see the three of you walking around town, but I suppose that's the nature of life, isn't it?" She caught sight of the clock and jumped. "Goodness. I've got to get back to the inn. Haven't even gotten my meat ordered yet." She nodded to PJ. "If you get to feeling bad again, I'll save a bit of crumble for you."

"Thanks, Bev." He closed his eyes, ready to sleep. "I'll do that."

~

Bev hurried back to the inn, but grabbed another bowl of crumble before heading across to the butcher shop. As before, Ida wasn't there, and Bev had to assume she was still very ill. But Vellora and Andres had returned, looking sunburnt and happy as Vellora dressed the pig on the hook.

"Afternoon, Bev," Vellora said. "Oh, what do you have there?"

"Tonic for your wife," Bev said. "Do you want to run it up to her?"

If Vellora had questions, she didn't ask them, merely taking the offered food from Bev and walking up the stairs. Bev turned to Andres, who also didn't seem to question why a tonic was in the form of a berry crumble, and nodded.

"Have you been enjoying your visit to Pigsend?" Bev asked.

"It's certainly not the trip I envisioned, but it's been enjoyable," he said. "Vellora might've been my subordinate, but we had a close bond throughout the war. She has a good eye for things, you know? Usually a pretty level head. Good instincts. If I ever questioned what to do, I'd run it by her, and she'd set me straight."

Bev warmed at the praise for her friend. "I confess, I've grown to love the two of them. Ida welcomed me to Pigsend the first day I arrived. In fact, she's a big reason Wim Mckee hired me to work at the inn in the first place. Then Vellora showed up a few months later, and one could see the sparks flying immediately."

"They do make a good pair," he said. "So, I know we touched on it when we chatted a few days ago, but…that first day you arrived in town. You really remember nothing?"

"There are feelings. Fragments. I know I wasn't supposed to stay here, but something kept me in place," Bev said. "And I had a pretty nasty gash to my head, that's it. That's all I know."

"Not even your birthday?" Andres said. "Your name?"

"Bev is a shortened version of Beverage Wench," Bev said with a laugh. "As for my birthday, Wim actually used to celebrate my birthday on the day I'd showed up. Haven't celebrated it since he died. Maybe I should restart the tradition, but it always fell on the anniversary of the war ending, so it felt a bit like we were celebrating that instead of me."

"And where do you stand on that?" Andres asked. "The war ending?"

Bev didn't quite understand the question, but before she could ask him to clarify, the door swung open behind them. Zed, Ollie, and Casimir stormed in, all looking angrier than Bev had ever seen them.

"Andres Rade!"

"Oh, goodness." Andres rolled his eyes. "What now?"

"You're under arrest," Zed said, pointing his finger at the other man.

"For what?" Bev asked, resisting the urge to roll her eyes with Andres.

"He *stole* my potions!"

CHAPTER TWELVE

For a moment, no one spoke.

"What potions?" Andres said with a frown.

But Bev's brows rose as she remembered the chest that Zed had procured to change his horses back to normal. "The whole chest?"

Zed nodded, his chest heaving.

"It hasn't been transformed into something else, has it?" Bev asked. "Like your horses were?"

"There's nothing in the tent," Zed said, coming closer. "*Someone* stole them. Probably so they can continue to cause mischief. Or potentially aim for the killing blow."

"It wasn't me, if that's what you're insinuating," Andres said. "I've been with Vellora all day."

"What's going on?" Vellora and Ida had come down, the latter looking like she'd eaten all the crumble and perked right up. Vellora quickly crossed the room, as if to stand between her former commander and potential jailer. "What do you want, Zed?"

"There's been another crime," he said, eyeing her suspiciously as Ida came to stand next to Bev. "Someone broke into our camp and stole my protective potions."

"Surprised a soldier fighting for the queen has such a thing," Vellora said coolly. "Outlawed for the rest of us, but okay for you? Seems fair."

"Vel," Ida said with a warning look.

"This whole town is full of jackals," Zed said. "Very well. I have ways of looking for magic without my potion. If you're as innocent as you say, neither one of you should show up with any traces of magic on your fingers."

Ida stiffened beside Bev.

Zed pulled out a roll of cloth and unfurled it on the counter. There were scissors, small knives, and a collection of long pins, one of which he pulled and examined before handing it to Ollie. "If anyone's been in contact with magic in the past few hours, this will tell." He turned to Andres. "You first."

He stepped up and offered his hand without complaint. Bev could practically hear the pounding of Ida's heart beside her, and hoped against hope that the crumble was effective enough to dilute the magic in her blood.

Ollie pricked Andres's finger, and a drop of blood came out. He flipped the pin and dabbed the head into it, then watched. Bev hadn't a clue what they were looking for, but when Zed's face screwed up in anger, she had to assume it had found nothing.

"Next," Zed thumbed toward Vellora.

"Why do I have to be tested?" Vellora asked.

"Because I said so," Zed said.

Vellora stepped forward and offered her hand. Once again, Ollie pricked it and tested the head against her blood. There seemed to be a longer wait this time, or maybe Bev was dreading the next question.

"You." Zed nodded to Ida. "You're up."

"My wife's been in bed sick the past few hours," Vellora said, unable to contain the small amount of panic in her voice. "She couldn't have stolen anything."

"Then she'll have no problem getting tested," Zed said. "Come. We don't have all day."

Ida stumbled forward, her face pale and sweaty once more. She extended her shaking hand and bit her lip so hard Bev was sure it was going to draw blood there. The blossom of blood appeared on her delicate finger, and Ollie touched the pinhead to it.

There was a collective inhalation of breath, or

perhaps that was the noise in Bev's head.

"Clean."

"What?" Ida blinked then, almost too late, plastered on a nervous smile. "I-I mean, of course. I haven't touched magic in…Well, ever, really. At least not intentionally. Probably wouldn't know it if I saw it. I—"

"Darling," Vellora said through clenched teeth as she pulled Ida back across the room.

"Right." Ida cleared her throat, hiding behind her wife.

"What about Bev?" Casimir asked.

"You know I had nothing to do with it," Bev said. "I was here putting in my meat order."

"And bringing crumbles, it seems," Zed said.

Bev tilted her head. "Pardon?"

"I saw you walking around town with bowls of something sweet," he said. "Such a kind gesture. It's not the solstice yet, though."

"Just testing out recipes," Bev said. "There's so much delicious fruit out there. Thought I'd make some to help Ida get back on her feet."

Zed scrutinized her. "Have any more? I'd *love* to try it."

⁓

Bev wasn't so naive to think Zed wanted to try her rhubarb crumble because he enjoyed them. There was a definite tension between him, Ollie, and Casimir. As the group walked into the front room of the inn, Kemp jumped to his feet, the book he'd been reading slamming shut.

"Ms. Bev! Are you all right? Are you under arrest for something?"

"No, Kemp," Bev said. "The soldiers wanted to try a bit of the crumble I've made, that's all."

"With the willow bark?" He made a face. "I tried some. It's acrid."

"Thank you, Kemp," Bev said, wishing once more that this man would *move on* from the inn, lest he get her into trouble.

"Willow's an odd choice," Zed said as they walked into the kitchen. "Not usually something one adds to baked goods. At least, Fernley never did."

Biscuit, who'd been sleeping under the table, lifted his head in concern, but at least had the good sense to keep his growling to himself.

Bev thought quickly. Andres's comment about soldiers arresting people for using herbs the wrong way stuck out in her mind, so she didn't want to mention the pain-relieving aspects. Nor did she want to mention anyone was feeling off, in case he wanted to know who to investigate further.

"Helps counterbalance the tartness from the rhubarb," Bev said, after a moment. "Wim told me about it."

"Hm." He walked to the half-eaten crumble and picked a rhubarb piece from the lot. He inspected it closely, as if it were a gem or a firework ready to explode. Then he popped it into his mouth. He chewed thoughtfully. "Metallic."

"Erm, yeah." Bev rubbed the back of her head. "The rhubarb had been in Herman's basement a while. Might not have been the freshest." She cleared her throat and gestured toward the other soldiers. "Would you like a bowl?"

"No," Zed answered for them. "What I'd like is to find my potions."

"Well, maybe I can help," Bev said. "How did it happen? Surely, you were guarding the camp after what happened to the caterpillars. Were they in your tent or…?"

Zed's murderous glare clamped her mouth shut. "I don't need your help investigating, Bev."

"Right, sorry." Bev smiled bashfully. "Just not used to someone solving their own problems. Usually, I'm the one who gets roped into it."

"And why is that, I wonder?" Zed asked, looking back at his two soldiers. "You have a sheriff in town, don't you?"

Rustin was sheriff in name only, but Bev didn't want to disparage him. "Rustin can be busy with… different things, you know. Sometimes these little quirky curiosities are beneath him."

"Like that woman cursing my son's wedding?" Zed asked. "Why didn't you have him handle that? Or tell him what you knew? Seems like you're good at keeping secrets, too."

She clicked her tongue at him. He certainly was a far cry from the jovial man who'd arrived at the inn a few weeks ago. "If you'd like to test me, you're welcome to. But I daresay you're better off working *with* me than against me. I'm trying to help, Zed."

"Are you? How are you helping?"

Bev couldn't tell him about the crumble, so she thought quickly. "I'm…trying to figure out what's causing the magical river to overflow. It seems more than the usual, even with the full moon."

He narrowed his gaze. "How do *you* know about the magical river?"

"Because when Karolina Hunter came to town, she stopped it from flowing and caused all the earthquakes and sinkholes," Bev said, matter-of-factly. "Another thing I had to solve because no one else would."

"So you know where this river runs in town?" Zed asked, almost thoughtfully.

"Somewhat," Bev said. "Just follow the sinkholes."

"Hm." He surveyed her, and Bev got the distinct impression his opinion was shifting about her. "You know, I think you may be on to something. There's certainly more magic around than usual, and it's making our job harder."

Bev nodded, relaxing a little.

"Well, I have no doubts you'll come to a suitable

answer soon," Zed said with a smirk. "Tomorrow, I want you to walk the path of the river, looking for anything suspicious. I expect a full report of your findings tomorrow at sundown."

~

Bev was a little miffed that Zed thought he could snap his fingers and she'd do what he said, but she *hadn't* yet walked the length of the river looking for anything suspicious, so it was a fine next step. Not to mention it would give her an excuse to find more afflicted Pigsend folk and offer them some of her crumble. Seeing Zed test Ida so quickly for magic had scared her more than she wanted to admit, and there were more folks in town who needed a slice of crumble to be safe.

Bev spotted Allen across the street, and while she still wasn't sure if it was his magic or Lillie's in the pastries, she wanted everyone with a speck of magic to have some iron, just in case. She crossed the street with a bowl in hand, finding Allen stirring a large bowl of fruit. Flour smeared his face and apron, but he smiled when Bev walked in the door.

"Oh, hey, Bev." Allen stopped and wiped his brow with the back of his hand. "What's going on? What do you have there?"

"I made, erm, a strawberry rhubarb crumble," Bev said. "Thought you might like some."

He made a face. "I'm full up on sweets, Bev. Couldn't possibly stomach another thing. But I did want to see if you could taste these muffins for me. I got new flour from Sonny. Want to make sure it's clear of magic."

Bev took a bite and knew immediately there was magic in them. To tell Allen and break his heart or not? She chewed thoughtfully, weighing the benefit of protecting his heart with keeping his father from finding out that he'd finally started showing his mother's magic.

"Ah, Bev, you're here!" Lillie walked through the door.

"Feeling better?" Allen asked.

"Much." Lillie winked at Bev. "Got some tonic from Bev, and all is right in the world."

"I was testing to see if there was magic in this flour," Bev said, offering another piece to Lillie.

She took a bite, giving Bev a sideways look then smiled at Allen. "Nope! All clear here." Lillie winked at Bev and took the muffin from her, breaking off another piece. "See for yourself."

Bev took a bite and found it void of any of the extra deliciousness. "Ah, you're right. All clear."

"Allen, why don't I take over for the rest of the day?" Lillie said. "I'm right as rain. You have some of that crumble and tell Bev what you think it needs. I had some earlier, but I'm not sure what's missing."

"*You're* not sure?" Allen said with a laugh.

"You've got a better palate than me right now,"

Lillie said. "Go on. Give it a bite."

Allen popped a strawberry into his mouth. "Well, first of all, what did you bake it in? I can taste something acrid."

"The rhubarb wasn't the freshest," Bev said with a bit of a frown. "Anything else?"

"Maybe a touch of lemon?" he said. "I don't know, it's hard to get around the metal." He ran his tongue along his teeth. "I need to grab a glass of water. Be back in a moment."

He disappeared through the back door, and Lillie stifled a giggle. "Well, that answers that. Not to mention the blueberry—"

Bev nodded. "I still don't think we should tell him. But that crumble should keep him from getting into any trouble with his father."

She told Lillie about the magic-detecting pin, and the color drained from Lillie's face.

"That was close," Lillie said. "You should serve that crumble to everyone in town, then. Just in case."

~

Bev certainly planned to, although she'd managed to waste most of the day. She headed across the street to the butcher shop, as she *still* hadn't put in her meat order. Ida and Vellora were in the back, talking in low voices. They visibly jumped when the bell over the front door dinged.

"Just me," Bev said. "Need to feed my guests

this evening, as it turns out."

"What did you put in that crumble?" Ida asked with a smile. "I can barely even lift a pig!"

"Willow and iron," Bev replied. "It's temporary, so your strength should return soon. I'm glad it worked."

"You and me both," Vellora said. "Can't believe that Zed. Testing us like we're common criminals. If I hadn't thought it would make him *more* suspicious, I would've thrown him out of the shop."

"Better to keep him happy," Bev said. "This will all blow over after the solstice. We need to keep our collective heads down until then."

"And eat more crumble," Ida said. "It was good. Just had a hint of metal, you know? You'll give Allen a run for his money in baking if he's not careful."

"I'll leave that baking to him and Lillie," Bev said with a chuckle. "I'm so sorry you and Andres keep getting caught up in Zed's schemes. But…you didn't steal his potions, did you?"

"*Of course not*," Vellora all but bellowed. "Do you think I'd be so stupid as to put my wife in danger? We haven't set foot at his camp since he arrived. Trying to run my business and transport my goods. Maybe even spend time with an old friend. Is that a crime?"

"No," Bev said with a firm nod. "It's your right. I was just asking." She paused, rubbing the back of her neck. "But you haven't seen anything…odd on your travels, have you? Are other farms farther out experiencing the same overabundance of fruit and vegetables?"

"Not as much, no," Vellora said, after pausing a moment. "It's worse the closer you get to the farmers' market on the west side of town. But, of course, that's where that Karolina Hunter put the anti-magic device, didn't she? Probably a large concentration of magic there."

Bev nodded. "That's my first stop tomorrow, the farmers' market and farms out there. Probably going to bring some crumble, too, in case anyone's suffering. But first..." She sighed, realizing once again she'd been distracted. "I do need some meat. Whatever you've got that's quick."

"Sausage?" Ida said.

"Perfect."

~

Though Bev wasn't looking forward to making dinner in the already-hot kitchen, at least sausage wouldn't take that long, and the bread was already baked. It had been a *very* long day, from getting up early and going to Merv's, then fighting Rosie's chickens, then making the crumble...the more she thought about it, the more tired she became. And tomorrow would be just as busy. She knew of a few people on the west side of town who had inklings of magic or had magical inclinations. Bathilda Wormwood, for one, and Ramone Comely, the sculptor who lived a few doors down.

But all thoughts of tomorrow screeched to a halt as a large globe of white light danced by her head. In fact, the street was full of them, differing sizes and shapes, floating around as if suspended in water.

Chapter Thirteen

"Well, what the heck is it?"

In virtually no time at all, every citizen of Pigsend had come out onto the street, gazing at these strange glowing balls that had appeared out of nowhere. The younger children giggled as they chased the orbs as if they were common bubbles, and the older folk scratched their heads and pointed at them.

Sheriff Rustin had been summoned, not by Bev, but by the confused shrieks coming from the other citizens of Pigsend. The sheriff, who'd been suspiciously absent since Zed had come to town, poked at one of the glowing balls with his finger. It shimmied as if amused and bounced away.

"I've never seen anything like this before in my life," Earl said, holding his hands out to catch one of the balls. It landed softly then bounced away.

"Where's Bardoff when you need him?" Etheldra drawled with more than a little sarcasm.

"He's off studying in Queen's Capital," Bev said. Biscuit was by her side, awoken from his crumble-induced nap, and sniffed the air as if it were filled with freshly cooked bacon. His tail wagged so fast it almost disappeared. Definitely magical.

Allen came to join her, watching the bouncing balls with glee. "What a solstice, eh? Has anyone figured out what these are?"

Bev turned back toward the Weary Dragon, wondering why her long-term guests hadn't yet come out to see the excitement. Was it because they knew what was happening?

"Calm down, calm down." Zed strode down the street, his shiny boots reflecting the bright orbs. "Everyone go back to your houses. We'll be sure to handle this."

"What is *this*?" Allen asked, clearly the only one in town who could talk back to someone like Zed.

Zed turned to his son, who Bev wasn't sure he'd actually seen since he'd been back, and cleared his throat. "Nothing to concern yourselves with. We'll clean all this up. You'll be able to return to your evening activities in no time. But we will need you to clear out so we can work."

"How are you going to work if you don't have your potions?" Bev asked.

Zed glared at her, and a blush rose to her cheeks. She probably shouldn't have volunteered that information, but it had come out before she could stop it.

"I'm well-versed in how to undo magic," he said.

"I'm sure you are." Andres stood off to the side with Vellora, the latter staring at the orbs with a wondrous smile. Andres, on the other hand, had his stone-cold stare fixed on Zed. "How are we to be sure *you* aren't the cause of this?"

"And why would we cause this?" Zed asked.

Andres lifted a shoulder. "Since you won't tell the townspeople what *this* is, what's to stop them from guessing that you're responsible?"

Bev squinted at him. It certainly sounded like he was stirring the pot. And if he was hoping to avoid suspicion that he was in town to cause the queen's people trouble, he wasn't succeeding.

"I'll tell you what they are," Max said, his old voice cutting through the tension like a knife. "They're balls of pure magic. A natural phenomenon when there's too much concentrated, and it breaks free like this."

Zed eyed Max suspiciously. "How do *you* know about that?"

"Dear Zed, in case you forgot, there used to be a plethora of learned magical people living in Pigsend," Max said, his voice unusually tight. "And though Her Majesty's forces have tried to eradicate them, their knowledge does live on in the minds of others."

It was, perhaps, a dangerous thing to admit, and Bev found herself holding her breath at the thought of her beloved librarian being hauled away for too much knowledge of magic.

"Just a random fluke!" Mayor Hendry arrived, looking much healthier than she had earlier in the day. She walked right up to Zed and nodded at him approvingly. "Mayor Jo Hendry, I don't believe we've met."

"Zed Mackey," he said.

"Oh, you're *Allen's* father," she said, as if she hadn't known that a month ago. Then again, she *had* skipped the blessed event entirely. Perhaps weddings weren't her thing. "It's a wonderful gift to Pigsend to have you back among us."

"Can you please assist me in getting all these people back into their homes?" Zed asked. "I can't have them milling about as we're trying to do our job."

"Of course, of course." Hendry turned and clapped her hands. "Everyone, I promise Commander Mackey has things under control. After all, he's one of us, isn't he? Yes, we're so proud that you've managed to make something of yourself in Queen's Capital." She patted him on the shoulder, seemingly oblivious to the dubious looks of Max and others. "Now, let's all do as the man says and scatter on home. Bev, aren't you about to serve dinner? Yes, Max, you look like you're in need of a meal."

On and on she went, walking through the crowd and naming everyone personally. It didn't escape Bev's notice that her powers of persuasion had been muted, and it took more than her usual cajoling to get everyone to listen. But, as Zed stood watching her warily, Bev concluded that was probably a good thing.

~

Bev did have dinner to cook, and several of the townsfolk who'd been standing around watching the globes came to the inn to eat. Or, more accurately, to stand at the inn's windows and comment on the soldiers' varying degrees of success with the magical orbs.

"Oh, almost got it," Stephen said, leaning against the glass. "Oof. Right on his face."

"Bless them. They sure are trying," Feliciano said.

Bev wasn't sure what she'd expected the soldiers to do, but throwing nets at the orbs wasn't it. The little orbs seemed mischievous, giggling as they bounced by the inn's windows and out of reach of the soldiers.

"What do you think they'll do with them once they catch them?" Bev asked Stephen.

"Oh, magic in that form is quite potent," he said. "Probably bring it back to the queen. She'd be over the moon to get it, I'm sure."

"And do what with it?" Bev asked. "I thought she didn't like magic."

"She doesn't like anyone *else* to have magic," Stephen said with a look.

Kemp bristled from the armchair. "Is dinner almost ready? I'm starving."

"Right, sorry." Bev glanced at the clock. It was nearly six, and she hadn't even started it. Luckily, sausage cooked well on top of the stove. "Getting it right now."

She got the stove fire going, and within no time, had sliced sausages frying up in the pan, along with potatoes and herbs. It wouldn't be the most robust meal she'd made, and she had to serve it in stages, as she couldn't get all the sausage in the pan together, but at least she got it done. She supposed she could be forgiven for being a little late with the meal, especially after the long day she'd had.

After the first round of sausage and potatoes went out to the hungry diners, she returned to the kitchen to cook the second round. But as soon as she set foot in the kitchen, she stopped short.

A single magical orb was bouncing in her

kitchen. Bev was entranced by it, and the sensation that it was something *more*, something powerful. Something that might break everything loose if she reached out and touched it.

But before she could, Biscuit jumped in the air and snapped it, swallowing it whole. His golden eyes lit up brightly for a moment, and his whole body shimmered as the orb seemed to move through him. Then the light went out, and he sat, licking his lips as if she'd fed him a morsel of beef.

"That's one down," Bev said with a shake of her head. "Wonder how they'll get on with the rest of them."

Based on the dancing lights outside the inn's windows as she brought out the second round of dinner, not very well. The first round had been devoured, and Kemp was first in line to get seconds. He piled his plate high and dashed to one of the far-off tables.

Stephen and Feliciano, still chuckling to themselves at the soldiers' misfortunes, were next. Solan simply hummed to themselves, as if globes of floating light occurred every day. Andres, to his credit, kept his wisecracks to himself and settled at the last empty table.

Etheldra, Earl, and Max came next, tittering about the globes and what they meant and how they seemed to be vexing Zed.

"Serves him right," Etheldra said. "Lording

about as he is. He's a farm boy dressing up as a soldier, if you ask me."

"A turncoat farm boy," Andres offered.

Etheldra cast him a long look. "I think we've heard enough from you today."

Bev had to hide her smile as Andres's brows rose in surprise. Vellora probably hadn't warned him about Etheldra.

"Good to see you're back to your usual self," Bev said as Etheldra plucked three slices of rosemary bread out of the basket.

"And good to see you've realized it's entirely possible to bake bread in the summer," she said, waving the third slice in Bev's face. "Really now. Wim used to bellyache about the weather, but I thought you were made of stronger stuff. And look at this: perfectly risen and baked bread."

She continued, earning an amused smile from Bev, as Earl came up to Bev. "Erm, she really is back to her—"

"I know," Bev said gently. Etheldra must not have told him what Bev had done. "And I'm glad to have her back to normal. I know you are, too."

He nodded. "I felt awful leaving this morning, but Hendry said she'd flay me alive if there weren't fireworks. Can't say no to paid work, especially after being gone for so long." He rubbed his forehead. "But erm, you think we're still having a solstice celebration? What with all this…excitement?"

"I have no doubt the soldiers will..." There was a loud crash outside, and the telltale sound of someone yelping in pain, along with another yell of annoyance. "They'll figure it out. After all, it's what they're here to do, isn't it?"

Earl looked like he wanted to say something else, but Etheldra barked at him to quit holding up the line, and he quickly joined her at the table.

"Good thing you were here to explain it all to us," Bev said to Max as he took Earl's place. "Have you actually seen anything like that before?"

He cracked a smile. "Once. Far away from here, in a place frequented by wizards and witches and other magical creatures. The presence of so many magical creatures brought it forth from the earth."

"You didn't mention *that* to Zed," Bev said.

"Well, I didn't think it wise to have him wander the town looking for magical creatures," Max said. "Goodness knows we have our share of folks who'd rather keep those abilities a secret. The solstice is doing funny things, and they're compounding." He paused, leaning closer. "Did you figure out what's going on with the river yet?"

"Not yet," Bev said. "I got...waylaid."

"And have you been able to figure out who turned the horses to insects?" Max asked.

Bev shook her head. She'd have to guess it was the same people who stole Zed's potions. But she had enough on her plate keeping the people of

Pigsend from succumbing to the river's effects, so Zed would have to solve that problem on his own.

"They'll turn up sooner or later, I'm sure," Bev said.

"Quite a dangerous game they're playing," Max said with a look.

"I could say the same for you, speaking up as you did," Bev said. "You've got to be more careful. Zed's a high-ranking soldier, you know. He could as easily arrest you for speaking about magic as for having it."

He puffed out his chest. "Be happy to be arrested for sharing knowledge. Can't imagine a better reason to go to jail."

With that, he took his plate and joined Stephen and Feliciano. Bev eyed the three of them, wondering what kind of "learned conversations" they were having now. Previously, Max had been quietly rebellious, his antics limited to keeping illegal books, but since those two had shown up, he seemed to have grown a bit more spine—and Bev wasn't sure that was a good thing.

Dinner continued rather uneventfully, save the globes bouncing outside the window. Every so often, one would smack against the window, giggle, then bounce away. Bev kept stealing glances at Biscuit, who was prowling the room in search of scraps and crumbs. He'd devoured that small magical ball, as his breed was designed to do, but the ones outside seemed so alive and with minds of their own, Bev wouldn't be surprised if he coughed it up later.

"Another delectable meal," Andres announced, handing over his empty plate. "You do run a great service here, Bev. Vellora's lucky to be so near."

"I hope your stay's been pleasant," Bev said. "Despite, erm…well, you know."

"Vellora's got quite the expansive route," he said. "We left at the crack of dawn and went this way and that, north and south and east and west. I doubt we stopped, even for a minute." He chuckled, thumbing toward the door. "Though Zed was *very* interested in getting a list of every farmer we visited. Wouldn't be surprised if he sent one of his soldiers to speak to every one."

"You can't blame him," Bev said. "His potions have gone missing now, too. Definitely enough to make a man paranoid someone's out to get him."

"I haven't been anywhere near his campsite," Andres said. "Couldn't even tell you where it is, to be honest. I'm sure Vellora's avoiding it at all costs." He yawned. "I believe it's going to be another long day tomorrow, so I'm going to retire."

"Are you going on deliveries again?" Bev asked. "Surely, you could spend a day here at the inn."

"I believe it's better if I have a rock-solid alibi," he said with a weary laugh. "As long as Zed's in town, it's in my best interests to spend as much time *away* from it as I can."

Bev couldn't argue with that and let him walk up the stairs. Yet again, Max, Stephen, and Feliciano left together, though this time, Max led them through the back door to avoid the soldiers still trying to catch the magical orbs. Solan and Kemp were the last to leave, the latter asking if there was anything he could do to help tidy.

"I wouldn't dream of asking you to help," Bev said with a wave of her hand. "I've been doing this a long time. You go upstairs and enjoy your stay."

But Kemp didn't move, instead casting a nervous look at the staircase. "I heard from some of the folks in town that you're the one who tends to handle the—*ahem*—local curiosities."

"Wish I didn't have that reputation, but yes, sometimes those things fall to me," Bev said. "We do have a sheriff, but—"

"I don't want to cause anyone undue stress," he said. "But there's a forest north of town that seems quite…wicked."

The dark forest certainly lived up to that name, and she could only imagine what it was doing with all the excess magic around. "Yes, I'd steer clear. It can have a mind of its own."

"That's it." He glanced at the stairwell again, as if deciding whether he wanted to continue. "Solan, is it? The one in the room next to mine."

Bev nodded. "Yes?"

"Well, earlier today, I was out for a walk before

it got too hot," he said. "And I saw them walking out of the forest."

"Really?" Bev asked.

He nodded. "There are other strange things, too. Odd smells coming from their room. Some rhythmic banging and chanting. It sounds like they're..." He looked both ways. "Casting some kind of magic in there."

"I'll be sure to look into it," Bev said.

He scampered up the stairs, almost as if he might spill more secrets if he stayed another minute. Bev watched him go, still unsure of his motives or reasons for staying in town. He seemed nice enough, but sometimes the nicest ones hid the deepest secrets.

Chapter Fourteen

Bev didn't know what to make of the information Kemp had given her. Solan was a bit strange, to be sure. They were certainly in tune with the magic floating about, but was their odd behavior because of the magic or were they always like that? The dark forest *was* a cresting point of the magical river, too, so Bev would have to pop over there sooner or later.

But all that would have to wait, as there were morning chores to do. As she walked out to feed Sin, one of those magical orbs came floating into the backyard. Bev watched it, feeling that same urge to touch it but keeping her hands to herself.

It was a good thing, too, because moments after

the orb appeared, Zed showed up with a bag, which he tossed over it. The orb shrieked with anger and thrashed in the bag, but whatever it was made of held it without trouble.

"Last one." He wiped his brow wearily. "I hope."

"You must be exhausted," Bev said. "Were you and your soldiers at it all night?"

He nodded. "Glad we were in town to handle things. Who knows what would've happened had someone touched one of those orbs?"

What indeed? "We're certainly grateful for your help," Bev said. "Allen should be by soon with muffins. Would you care to stay and—"

"No, I've got to get back to camp and regroup," he said. "Probably going to pay that librarian a visit today. He seems to know a bit more than is good for him."

"Max is harmless," Bev said, waving Zed off.

"Ideas turn into action, if given enough water," Zed said.

Bev sighed. "Zed, what is going on? You weren't nearly this jumpy at the wedding a few weeks ago. What's changed?"

Zed worked his jaw. "I've got it under good authority that there *is* something nefarious going on in Pigsend. While yes, magical rivers do crest during full moons, *someone* is taking advantage of it to hide their own magical abilities. A wizard, perhaps, or even a mage. Someone who can't walk down the street without being noticed."

Bev had considered that. "To what end, though?"

"I told you we were monitoring rebellious activity in town," Zed said. "What I didn't tell you is we believe there'll be a meeting of like-minded individuals sometime in the next few days. They intend to take their plans to the next step, which may include launching an attack on Queen's Capital."

Bev wiped her hands on her apron. Zed surely knew more about these things than Bev, but she had a hard time believing anyone in town would be capable of that.

His next question was almost reading her mind. "I'll ask you again: have you noticed anything from your guests, other than Andres?"

"No, Zed," Bev said with a sigh. "They're all…" Well, she couldn't say "normal." Stephen and Feliciano could certainly be accused of wanting to plot against the queen. Kemp seemed to notice a bit too much of everything. Solan was…well, they were on their own level. But capable of overthrowing the queen? That seemed a step too far. "I have nothing to report in that area."

"Well, if that changes, you know where to find me." He tipped his head at her as he threw the magical orb over his shoulder. "I'll be by later to find out what you've learned about the magical river.

Don't disappoint me."

"What are you doing with those orbs?" Bev found herself asking. She didn't know why—it wasn't as if she wanted to be anywhere near them.

"They'll be dealt with appropriately," he said. "Where they can't be used against Her Majesty or her forces."

He huffed, as if to drive home his point, before turning on his heel and leaving Bev alone in the backyard.

~

Bev would've been lying if she said she wasn't unnerved by her conversation with Zed. It certainly explained his change in demeanor, and why the mere presence of Andres had made his blood boil. Rebellions and wars seemed like concepts too big for a simple innkeeper to understand. From Pigsend, Queen Meandra was a far-off figure, someone talked about but never seen. The war was something in the past that haunted Vellora and that had changed the makeup of Allen's family, but here in Pigsend, the only concerns were the next rainfall and the annual Harvest Festival.

But the outside world had been creeping into Pigsend, starting with Karolina Hunter all those months ago. And Bev was wondering if soon, the sleepy farm life of this town would also become a thing of the past.

She shook off those thoughts, which had settled

sad and hard in her chest, and waited for her guests to wake. She hadn't had any single-nighters (perhaps the glowing orbs had scared them off), so there were only her long-term guests to tend to. For the best, as she had another busy day ahead of her.

At seven, Lillie arrived with muffins. She had a spring in her step, too, which she attributed to the pot of tea she'd made for herself and Allen.

"I hid the kettle," Lillie said with a mirthful smile. "So all we had to boil water in was a big iron pot." She chuckled. "Hurt when I touched it, so I made Allen do it. Luckily, he didn't seem to catch on."

"Smart," Bev said.

"I was starting to feel poorly again," she said. "So I think it's something I'll have to do every morning. Not that I don't love having tea that tastes like iron." She made a face. "But if it keeps us safe..."

"I'm not sure it'll be enough," Bev said, with a concerned frown. "I think Allen would pass muster, but you've got so much..."

She cleared her throat, sounding a bit like she had when she'd first realized she was officially kicked out of Lower Pigsend. "Well, I made my bed, didn't I? Suppose it'll be what it is. If Zed's on the hunt for magical folk—"

"That's the thing," Bev said. "I'm not sure they're looking for just anybody. This morning, Zed acted like he's hunting for someone trying to overthrow the queen."

"I doubt he'd find that out here, would he?" Lillie asked.

"He seems to think he will," Bev said with a sigh. "And now he wants *me* to walk around town and look for suspicious activity around the river. So that's what I'm doing today."

"Why can't he do it?" Lillie asked.

"Well, to be honest, I'd rather check it out myself," Bev said. "Because if I do see anything amiss, I might be able to put a stop to it before that person ends up in handcuffs."

"Who's going to end up in handcuffs?" Kemp, of course, stood at the top of the stairs.

Bev wasn't sure how much of the conversation he'd overheard, and gave a meaningful look at Lillie. "Just a figure of speech." Lillie quickly excused herself and scurried out the door. "Did you have a good night, Kemp?"

"Kept glancing out the window, looking for those orbs," he said, adjusting his shirt. "Have they…erm…disappeared?"

"I think so," Bev said. "Here, have a muffin. Lillie's dropped them off."

"That was one of the bakers?" He cleared his throat. "Oh, I wish you would've introduced me. I have some questions for them."

"What kind of questions?" Bev asked, narrowing

her gaze.

"Well, these muffins are extraordinary," he said. "I'd like to know what's in them."

"We're having a banner year for produce."

"It's quite fortunate they're across the street," he said, picking up a muffin finally. "Maybe I can head over there—"

"Oh, they're very busy today," Bev said, hoping that would suffice. "Lillie's only just here for a moment. Overrun with pie orders. Solstice, you know?"

"Hm. Maybe after, then."

She exhaled when he turned to walk back up the stairs. It *would* be fitting if a queen's soldier arrived at the inn under a false name and snooped until they found something worth reporting. And Zed might not recognize the soldier, either, or know he was in town. The same thing had happened during the Harvest Festival, after all.

Soon enough, her attention was diverted by Feliciano and Stephen, who came down deep in conversation. They brightened when they saw the muffins, and seemed, at least, in a better mood than Kemp.

"Looks like those soldiers managed to get those lights under control," Feliciano said with an impish look. "Wonder if they used a tincture of willow? Much faster than trying to catch them one by one."

"Oh?" Bev tilted her head. Curious they would

mention willow. "Why?"

"It can help tame wayward magic," Stephen said. "Put it in a perfume bottle and spritz it in the air. Those orbs would've come right back down and behaved."

"I'm sure Zed must've had some in his potion kit," Bev said. "Unfortunately, someone seems to have taken it."

She watched for signs of guilt, but all she got was amusement from both men. "Oh, dearie me. What's a soldier to do without his protective potions?" Feliciano said with more than a hint of sarcasm.

Stephen chuckled. "Maybe if they hadn't run everyone who could make more out of the country, he might've found someone who could've helped."

"Maybe," Bev said, not quite sure if they were enjoying the misfortunes or the cause of them. "What are you two up to today?"

"Another stroll about town," Feliciano said. "We're so enjoying the variety of the plant life. Especially with everything in full bloom."

"Indeed." Stephen nodded emphatically. "I wonder, what's the story of that forest up north? It seems to be positively teeming with life."

"The dark forest? I'd steer clear," Bev said. "The very few times I've gotten tangled in it, I haven't enjoyed myself. It's full of...well, I'm not sure what, but not good things."

If either man heard her, they didn't show it, thanking her for her hospitality before bidding her farewell. Once again, Bev found herself pondering the motives of her guests—at least until the last of the bunch made their appearance. Still, none warranted a report to Zed. Not yet, anyway.

Of the three sets of guests, Solan looked the most aggrieved. Their long hair was flat and greasy, and their cheeks seemed much paler than usual. If Bev could imagine any of them having magic, it would be this interesting person. But was having magic a crime, or a coincidence?

"These muffins are the trick," Solan said weakly. "I really must thank the baker for his generosity."

Bev wanted to say that the cost of the breakfast was included in the gold paid but decided against it. "They're right next door."

They waved her off. "It's not right to leave this place. Not until the solstice is over."

But didn't Kemp say... "Really?" Bev asked, trying to keep her face passive. "Not even leaving the inn?"

"No, no." They picked up another muffin. "May I have another? They're so divine."

"Help yourself."

"I thought I heard chatter about a cobbler or crumble you'd made, too? I certainly smelled it bubbling away yesterday. I was hoping we might see it for dinner, but it wasn't on the spread. Is there any left? May I have a bite?"

"Sure," Bev said. Then, because she was curious how Solan would respond, she added, "I did bake it with iron and willow. For taste."

"Oh, you did?" They made a face. "Never mind, then."

Bev cleared her throat, wanting to press a little more. "That was certainly something about those orbs last night."

They stared back blankly. "Orbs?"

"Those floating light things?"

"Oh, right. The magic." They laughed. "It's sort of expected, isn't it?"

"Is it?" Bev smiled. "It's never happened around here before. At least, not in my memory. Why would you say it was expected?"

"The magic is so high," they said, as if discussing the weather. "It's practically humming on my skin. You can't feel that?"

"No, I can't say I do," Bev said.

"Hm." They shrugged as if that weren't anything interesting. "We must take care, though. If we aren't careful, we're likely to get a nasty magical storm out of all this."

"What's that?" Bev asked.

"Let's hope we don't find out, and whatever's causing the magic to act out will stop."

Bev wasn't sure Solan knew there were soldiers about, though she had to think they'd seen them walking about town. "Well, in any case, you may want to keep mum on the magical talk. Some of Her Majesty's folks are in town, and they don't usually like people talking about it." She paused. "In fact, they've been targeted by someone using magic, so they're a bit more on alert than usual. Better to keep your head down, you know?"

"Indeed, I do." Again, Solan was unbothered. "Well, I'd best be heading upstairs. Good day to you, Ms. Bev."

With a muffin in each hand, they sauntered up the stairs and were soon gone.

"Biscuit," Bev said, looking down at the laelaps. "I want you to stay here and keep an eye on Solan. If they go anywhere, come get me, okay?"

Ruff.

~

Not that Solan was a prime suspect, but there was certainly something off about them. That, or Kemp was telling lies. She thought about telling Biscuit to come get her if Kemp left, too, but decided against it for the moment. *If* someone was mucking up the river, she'd hopefully find the culprit and get some questions answered.

Said river was a bit hard to pin down. Bev wasn't exactly sure where it came into town and where it left, but she did know the places where it ran the highest. The dark forest, the inn, under the Brewer twins' house, near Rosie Kelooke's backyard, and the town square. Each spot where a sinkhole had caused devastation from the absence of magic.

Bev had walked this path once before using a divining stick, but if she used that stick now, it would probably send her all over the place. No use in trying to divine magic when it was so plentiful it was floating in midair.

But it was clear where the river ran and where it didn't. Much like at the farms in town, there was an overabundance of plant life that paved a clear path around town. Bev's herb garden, which she'd taken to cutting back every morning after she fed Sin, was already knee-high by midday. Rosie's yard was also overflowing with every color of blooms, even with the chickens eating them back as fast as they could grow. The town square was awash with green grasses and purple and pink bell flowers that swayed in the warm breeze.

Earl was there with hedge clippers, working on the bushes in front of the schoolhouse. Etheldra had mentioned he was at war with the bushes, and he seemed to be having the same difficulties Bev had with her garden. The carpenter waved as Bev approached then took off his cap and wiped his brow.

"All this heat sure is making these hedges grow," he said. "I cut these back yesterday, and this morning, they're overgrown."

Bev nodded. She wasn't sure how much

Etheldra had shared about magic and the secret magical life of things. Perhaps better to keep Earl in the dark on such matters, as it didn't affect him too much. "How are the solstice celebration plans going otherwise?"

"Well, I think," he said. "But if these hedges don't stay cut, it won't be safe to set the fireworks off. If I didn't think Bardoff would hunt me down for it, I'd cut them down at the root."

"That's what I have to do with my herb garden," Bev said. "It's the same story there. I think if you cut it down, it might grow back, though."

He sighed. "Well, that certainly is a pickle, isn't it?"

"Sure makes for more work," Bev said.

"Better to stay busy. Etheldra's back in her right mind, thanks to you, I hear," he winked, "but she's still in a foul mood today. Went to Shasta Brewer's house to get her to come back to work and Shasta declined. Acting all funny, too." He pushed his hat up on his head. "You know, Etheldra mentioned you should probably pay the girl a visit. Not sure why, but..."

Bev sighed. "I do."

Seemed another person in town needed some of her delicious crumble.

Chapter Fifteen

The Brewer house was a two-minute walk from the schoolhouse, made longer because Bev had to double back to the inn to retrieve a bowl. There was about half a pan of crumble left, and if things continued as they were, Bev would certainly have to make more. It seemed everyone in town had suddenly been struck by a spate of magical abilities —not the best development when a cadre of magic-testing soldiers were on the hunt.

Bev walked up the front steps, a single bowl in hand. Earl had rebuilt the twins' quaint house after the sinkhole fiasco, and it still looked new and freshly painted several months later. Bev knocked loudly on the door and stepped back.

The knob turned, and Shasta appeared, looking pale and red-eyed, like she'd been crying. "O-oh, Bev. Hello. I'm sorry, I'm a mess. Not in the mood for company right now."

"I've brought you a little treat," Bev said, holding up the bowl. "Thought it might cheer you up."

"Oh, is that..." She examined the contents of the bowl. "Well, that actually looks delicious." She sniffed back tears. "Come on in."

Bev stepped inside and found a nicely-decorated living room full of paintings of plants, pretty curtains with embroidered flowers, and blooms on almost every table. Herbs scented the air, as if Shasta were making her own teas even after being fired.

"So I hear Etheldra came by," Bev said.

Shasta screwed up her face and looked as if she were going to sob again. "*Don't* even say her name! The things she said... The way she treated me... She's always treated me poorly, but that was the last straw." Her lip quivered. "Especially after losing Vicky to Sheepsburg. It's all been too much lately."

Bev sat on one of the two chairs, patting the other one. "Have you heard from Vicky?"

"A few letters here and there," she said, taking the seat. "But it's not the same. We grew up together, you know? And now she's gone, and..." She sighed, rubbing her temples. "Sorry. My head hasn't been right for days."

"Maybe try a bit of the dessert," Bev offered.

Shasta took the bowl but didn't eat. "I've been so…off lately. Everything feels overwhelming."

"Does your sister feel the same?"

"She's still got *her* job." Shasta glared to the window, as if her sister was in the room. "Said we could work together there, but there's barely any room for her or Bernard, you know? Besides that…" She sighed. "I loved blending the teas. I don't know why Etheldra got so cross with me so suddenly. It's like…like she went mad!"

"She kind of did." Bev cleared her throat. "Have a bite of that. I want to know what you think."

Shasta made a face, as if she really didn't want to, but took a small bite. She chewed thoughtfully, making a face as everyone else with magic had, then blinked, looking down at it. "What's in this?"

"Why do you ask?"

"Because…" She looked up at Bev, as if she were about to divulge a horrible secret. "Well, I suppose… Um…"

A moment later, the front door opened. Stella came rushing in, her eyes wild and frantic as they scanned the room. She only heaved a sigh of confused relief when her gaze landed on her sister.

"What happened?" Stella asked her sister. "I can't hear you anymore."

"What do you mean?" Bev asked. "I can hear her fine."

"Not...out loud," Shasta said, her cheeks reddening.

"Ssh!" Stella snapped at her sister. "She'll think us mad."

"It's Bev," Shasta replied. "She probably already knows what's going on."

"I don't exactly," Bev said. "But it's all right. You can trust me."

The twins shared a glance before Stella quietly said, "Lately, my sister and I have been able to hear each other...in our minds."

Bev's eyes widened. That was a new one. "In your minds?"

"My sister and I have always had a... connection," Shasta said softly. "Knowing when the other was hurt, what the other was doing, that sort of thing. But the past few days—"

"It's been amplified?" Bev said.

They nodded.

"Do you have any magical blood in your family?" Bev asked.

"No," Shasta said.

"At least, not that we know of," Stella countered. "Though we did have Great Aunt Penelope."

"Did she have magic?" Bev asked.

"No, but she threw a right fit when our mother was pregnant with us," Shasta said. "Refused to let her back in the door. Mother never said what it was about, though."

"I always thought it was because she had us out of wedlock," Stella said.

"That's silly, because Cousin Wendy had three kids out of wedlock," Shasta said. "And she's still allowed to come to the solstice dinner every winter."

"True."

Bev cleared her throat. "So perhaps your father had it?"

"It's possible," Stella said. "But we certainly don't."

Stella shook her head. "At least, we haven't until being able to hear each other."

"I do think it's curious you and your sister opted for jobs with concoctions and brews," Bev said, after a moment's thought. "Etheldra's got a similar affinity. She says the plants were talking to her. They don't do that with you, do they?"

Shasta shook her head. "The only voice I've been hearing is my sister's."

Stella turned to Bev, concern etched on her face as she glanced out the window. "Don't go spreading that around town, will you?"

Bev held up her hands. "Not planning on it. That's honestly why I brought over the crumble." She gestured to the bowl still in Shasta's hands. "It's supposed to dull the effects of magic. The river is high right now, and it runs right beneath your house."

"Well, that explains a lot," Shasta said to her sister. "Here, have a bite."

"Is that why that earthquake—?" Stella asked Bev as she crossed the room to share with her sister.

Bev nodded. "Back then, the soldiers stopped the flow of magic, and the earth responded. Now, it's the opposite. Too much magic. I don't know if you saw those orbs of light last night, but—"

Shasta nodded. "I saw them on my way home. And I saw those soldiers running around trying to catch them, too. I don't like that Zed's back in town. He gave me the creeps at the wedding, and now he seems…"

Bev told them what she knew of his reason for being in town, and that he was on the hunt for someone out to cause real trouble.

At that, Shasta barked a laugh. "Who in Pigsend's going to overthrow the queen?"

"Who indeed," Bev said. "But until all this blows over, I've got to keep him from arresting everyone with a lick of magic."

"How are you going to do that?" Stella asked.

"Well, today, I'm walking the path of the magical river looking for trouble," Bev said. "And offering a bowl of crumble to anyone who might be afflicted. I'd given some to Ida a few moments before she was tested for magic, and she didn't show up as having any."

"What a frightening scenario," Shasta said. "You

know, you should probably give some to Etheldra."

"Already did," Bev said. "Which is why she asked you to come back to work."

"It wasn't so much asking as telling me I was late," Shasta said with a grimace. "But I told her if she thought I was coming back to be abused like that, she had another think coming."

"Yeah, but what else are you going to do?" Stella asked. "You won't come work with me at the apothecary."

Shasta's face reddened. "I'll figure something out."

"Give Etheldra another chance," Bev said. "She really wasn't in her right mind. And she felt awful when she came to."

"Is she capable of feeling awful?" Shasta asked. "I'm really not sure."

There was a knock at the front door, and the girls shared a look of concern. Before she crossed the room to the door, Stella took three more big bites of the crumble, and her sister finished the lot. Then she opened the door.

"Sheriff Rustin, good morning," Stella said, sounding unnerved.

"Hey, Stella, Shasta. Bev!" He brightened. "Well, good morning. I didn't expect to see you here."

"I heard Shasta needed a pick-me-up," Bev said. "I'd made this crumble yesterday and had lots left over."

"Why do you need a pick-me-up?" Rustin asked.

"Etheldra fired her," Stella said.

"Oh, that's a shame," Rustin said. "She's been heated lately, for sure. You know I try to avoid her when I can. Somehow I don't think—"

"Erm, Sheriff," Shasta said, her voice tight. "Is there something we can help you with?"

"Yeah. Gosh, this is awkward." He rubbed the back of his neck then reached into his pocket and pulled out a familiar roll of cloth. Zed's magical testing equipment. "You know Zed Mackey's in town, right? He's asked me to test some folks for magic. Had a big list of people. Including Etheldra, but you know I'm not going near her, so—"

"Why test us for magic?" Shasta said. "We don't have any."

"Well, someone said you two were acting squirrelly," Rustin said. "Like unable to hear? Talking to yourselves. It's all on the up and up, you know. Zed said he wants to help."

The three women shared a dubious glance.

"In any case, it's a quick test." He lifted his shoulder. "Well?"

"Rustin, I know you aren't bothering these ladies."

Rustin jumped almost a foot in the air and cast a terrified look behind him. Etheldra stood there, hands on her hips as she glared at him with the fire of a thousand suns.

"M-Ms. Etheldra. Didn't hear you walk up—"

"I'm sure you didn't, with your laborious mouth-breathing. What in the world are you doing here, bothering my employee and her sister?"

"Z-Zed told me—"

"I don't give a flying feather what that turncoat told you to do," Etheldra barked. "You'll be on your way, Sheriff, telling him you tested all three of us and found nothing, you hear?"

"But—"

She bared her teeth at him and he yelped, turning on his heel and dashing out of the house.

Shasta and Stella let out breaths of relief, and Shasta gave Etheldra a grateful smile. "Thank you for stepping in."

"You've had some of that crumble, yeah?" Etheldra said, nodding to the empty bowl. "Good. You'd probably be fine to be tested, but better not to tempt fate." She lifted her chin. "Now, I came here to talk with you about the shop."

"I told you," Shasta said with a sniff, "I'm not coming back. You're too mean."

"Stupid girl," Etheldra muttered with a shake of her head. "If you won't come back, then who am I going to sell it to when I retire next year?"

Shasta blinked, staring at her sister in surprise. "You were…going to sell it to me?"

"You were going to retire?" Bev said.

"Yes, and *maybe*, if I found someone I trusted to take over." Etheldra's pale cheeks had started to turn red. "And I thought it was *you*, girl."

"But you said—"

"Ignore what I said when my brain was addled with magic." Etheldra waved her off. "You're the only one with any affinity for tea mixing, save maybe your sister, but she decided to work with Bernard, didn't she?"

"I have some stipulations," Shasta said slowly.

"The stipulation is you get an entire shop and its contents," Etheldra said. "And you'll pay me royalties until you pay back the mortgage unless you can secure one from a bank yourself."

Shasta quirked a brow, and for the first time, perhaps Etheldra *wasn't* the most powerful person in the room.

"It'll be a fair price," Etheldra said, after a long pause. "Maybe take you a year to pay off. But Earl and I want to travel before we're too old to do so, and I can't give it to you for free."

Shasta shared a look with her sister, and Bev got the impression the two of them wished they had their mind-link back. Finally, Shasta rose and dusted off her skirt with painstakingly slow effort. Then she lifted her head, met Etheldra's gaze, and smirked.

"Fine. I'll come back to work. But if you're truly interested in selling to me, you *will* treat me as an equal partner in the shop. No more lording over me, insulting me, or ordering me around. Understand?"

Etheldra snorted.

"Understand?"

"Fine." She held out her hand. "Partners?"

Shasta shook it, and her sister burst into applause. "Oh, Shas, imagine what Vicky will say! A whole shop to yourself. You're going to do amazing things!"

Bev smiled but felt Etheldra's gaze on her as the twins celebrated. "What is it?"

"I'm surprised you're still here," Etheldra said. "As Rustin very clearly said, he was going around town testing people. Maybe you should catch up with him. Bring your crumble, too."

"But I've got—" Bev stopped. "You're right. Suppose I'd better go find him."

~

Rustin wasn't very far, walking down the road checking his list and mumbling to himself. When Bev called out to him, he turned with a bright smile.

"Hey, Bev! What a day, eh?"

"Where are you headed next?" Bev asked.

"Bathilda's house, all the way outside town!" He shook his head. "Not as if I didn't have other things to be doing today, but Zed insisted." He sniffed. "What am I doing anyway? Testing people for magic. No one in town *has* magic. But he wouldn't listen."

"He's pretty intent on finding the person who

turned his horses into caterpillars," Bev said. "And stole his potions." She craned her neck to take a look at the list. "Who all have you tested so far?"

"Well, no one. Everyone's sent me away," Rustin said. "And I didn't want to test Etheldra, because I knew she'd bite my head off. Thought I was being sneaky coming to the twins' house. Oh, well. What Zed doesn't know won't hurt him."

"Would you mind if I took a look at that sheet?" Bev asked. "Just to see if I've seen anything."

"Oh, sure." He handed it over.

She scanned the names, finding the ones he'd mentioned already, plus a few more. The Norrises were on the list, which made sense, considering Dag had almost pegged them as having a dragon shifter for a son. Bathilda Wormwood, who hadn't been seen in several days, Trent Scrawl, and a few others.

"This certainly sounds like a big job," Bev said. "Especially going to see Penelope Bridges. She lives all the way out near Middleburg."

He groaned. "You're right, she does. Can't imagine she's here causing trouble, but what do I know?" He sighed. "It's going to take me forever to get out there. Then I've got to head in the opposite direction to speak with Freddie Silver." He looked over the list again. "There's no way I can get this done today."

"Why don't I help?" Bev said, before she could stop herself. "At least the ones in town. I could go ask them questions. Zed wanted me to walk around anyway to find anything funny. Could do both at once. If I find anyone I think you should test, you can visit them later."

"Really?" Rustin brightened. "Oh, Bev. That would be wonderful. You have such a way with people."

"Happy to help," Bev said. "But you'd better get a move on if you want to make it to Penelope's house."

He adjusted his shirt. "I tell you what, I'll be happy when the solstice is over. Nothing but trouble it's been!"

"You said it."

Chapter Sixteen

Of course, Bev had no intention of telling Rustin or Zed anything, but every name on his list *also* happened to be where the magical river was highest, so she was happy to do it. She crossed the Norrises off the list, as she'd already delivered their crumble, and stopped by the inn to grab two more bowls for Ramone and Bathilda. Ramone seemed a likely candidate for magical abilities, as they'd seemed affected by their brother's absence and reappearance. But as she walked up the front steps to their home, there was a sign nailed to the door.

Gone north for the summer.

Kisses,

R.C.

"Good to know," Bev said, blowing air between her lips. The sculptor probably wouldn't be putting the dragon fountain back in the town square any time soon if they weren't coming back for the summer. But at least they wouldn't be bothered by Zed or the increase in magic.

She left the artist's house and continued down the dusty road. She kept her eyes peeled for anything suspicious, but she doubted she'd find anything out in the open like this. She gazed across the fields, looking for more of those globes that might've escaped Zed's capture, but nothing stared back except waving stalks of corn and full fruit trees. Maybe out here, the magic was being sopped up by the plants, and there wasn't enough of it to escape, like in town.

"A fine theory," Bev said to herself.

In the distance, she spotted the dark forest rising from the edge of Alice's farm. The magical river *definitely* went through there, but Bev was leery about venturing there alone. After all, it was bad enough during normal times. She didn't want to think about how dangerous it would be if she attempted it now.

Instead, she took a left and walked down a dirt path toward Bathilda's house. The last time Bev had been here, she'd been trying to find out to whom she'd sold her herd of magical sheep, but the farmer had been out of town. Alice had said she was back but acting strangely again. Bev prepared herself to be greeted by a crossbow, unsure which version of Bathilda she'd get today.

The woman who opened the door only came up to Bev's stomach, and her white hair seemed more frazzled than usual. Her apron had singe marks on it, as if she'd gotten too close to a candle. And on closer inspection, there were burn marks all over her arms and a few on her cheeks. While she looked somewhat put out to see Bev, thankfully, she wasn't wielding her crossbow.

"Morning, Bev," she said, closing the door behind her. "What can I do for you?"

"Are you all right, Bathilda?" Bev asked. "You look, well, I don't want to say a mess, but—"

"Fine." The tone made it clear she didn't want to discuss it. "What can I do for you?"

"Well, I'm sure you're aware there've been some interesting things afoot."

"Have there?" She raised an eyebrow, part of which was missing. "Nothing strange here. Best be on your way. Goodbye." She turned to walk back inside.

Bev cut right to the chase. "Yes, but the soldiers added your name to a list of possible magic users," Bev said. "And I'm here to see if you're suffering from the effects of the risen magical river."

She stopped mid-step then turned around. "What soldiers?"

"Zed Mackey, for one. Allen's father. I don't know if you—"

"I remember him. He left to fight for the king, didn't he?" Bathilda put her hands on her hips.

"He switched sides," Bev said. "In any case, he's in town looking for people causing trouble, and he's convinced someone's adding to the magic in town. So he's put together a list of people for Rustin to speak with."

"So why are you here?" Bathilda snapped.

"I took the list and told him I'd help," Bev said. "But you know, I'm not—"

"Yeah, I know." Bathilda softened a little. "Well, you said the magic river was high?"

Bev nodded. "Both from the solstice and full moon, but also—"

"That explains a lot, then." She rubbed a bald spot on the side of her head. "Just my luck."

"Bathilda, are you all right?" Bev asked. "Seriously. You don't have another strange creature in there, do you?"

She grimaced then beckoned Bev to follow her. Inside, her home shared her half-burned motif, with large, circular scorch marks all over. Her floral couch was half-destroyed, and it seemed all the other furniture had been reduced to ash.

"What happened in—"

A beautiful, golden-plumed bird floated down to land on the part of the couch that hadn't been burned. It was the most exquisite thing Bev had ever seen, with red streaks shimmering on its breast and beak. It lifted a wing and pruned itself, pulling out a few feathers before stretching its neck.

"Here we go," Bathilda muttered.

The creature's eyes bulged, as if something were caught in its throat. It squawked loudly, shuddering and shaking like it was seizing.

Then it exploded in a bright plume of fire, and the couch caught fire with it. Bathilda, clearly used to this exercise, went to the corner of the room, where several buckets were already filled with water. She methodically poured water onto the fire.

"Well, don't stand there and let my couch burn, Bev!" Bathilda barked.

Bev jumped, realizing she had two hands to help, and hurried over to pick up buckets. After four douses, the fire was out, but there was no saving the couch.

"I'm so sorry about your bird," Bev said, staring at the pile of ash where it had been. "It was so—"

Bev's words died when a small, ugly, featherless creature emerged from the ashes, squeaking and opening its jaws as if waiting for its mother to feed it.

"Now, you just ate," Bathilda said with a grimace, but she nonetheless walked to the kitchen to retrieve a jar filled with dirt and worms. She pulled one out and fed it to the bird, who chirped happily. A single red feather popped out from atop its head.

"What is this thing?" Bev finally managed.

"A phoenix," Bathilda said. "My cousin got me into them."

"The same cousin who told you the tanddaes would be a good investment?" Bev asked with a small laugh.

Bathilda didn't think it was funny. "I confess, I got a bit of the sales bug from the sheep, you know. Making that kind of money was wonderful. So I invested again. My cousin said, 'Don't worry, phoenixes are small. You can keep them in your house.'" She harrumphed. "This thing is about to burn down my whole house. Can't wait to be rid of it. But my buyer hasn't shown up. Late. Inconsiderate thing, he is."

"Probably trying to avoid the soldiers," Bev said gently. The Lower Pigsend people had a merchant who traveled the country for them, and he'd been the one to buy the sheep off Bathilda a few months ago. "But I'm not sure it's the wisest idea to have this thing fluttering around your house right now. If Zed should come knocking—"

She sniffed. "I won't let him in. Still have the ability to turn people away, don't I?"

Bev gave her a look.

"Well, there's not much I can do about it," Bathilda said, slumping into her chair. The phoenix, which had already sprouted more feathers and was hopping on the ground as if ready to take flight, popped over to her shoe and picked at the laces. "I'll say I've gotten into making fireworks for the solstice. Earl's still planning on that, isn't he? Or has Zed ruined that, too?"

"He is," Bev said. "But in the meantime, maybe…"

The phoenix burped, and a plume of fire came out, setting the rug on fire. Bathilda stamped it out immediately.

"Yeah, I won't be answering the door for anyone." She sniffed. "But if you happen to see anyone who looks like they could be in the market for a phoenix, maybe tell them to hurry it up and take this thing off my hands?"

~

Bev felt for Bathilda, although it seemed the farmer hadn't quite learned her lesson from the tanddaes, and her current predicament was her own doing. Still, it wasn't right for someone to be arrested simply for having magical creatures, either.

Before leaving the west side of town, Bev walked a bit of the dark forest. As predicted, it was more alive than ever, shivering and shaking when she stepped too close to the brambles. She didn't *see* anything out of the ordinary, save some curious-looking orange vines farther in. But there were all manner of interesting plants in the dark forest, and the vibrant vines were surely a reaction to the increase in magic.

She turned to head back to the inn but spotted activity at Herman Monday's farm. Two of Zed's soldiers were standing in his pumpkin patch, and it seemed from Herman's red face that the trio were arguing. Herman stood protectively in front of several green orbs that were already larger than any pumpkin had a right to be, maybe even bigger than the one that had won last year's Harvest Festival. She could see why the soldiers would think he was doing something underhanded.

"Ah, there's someone with a brain." Herman gestured toward Bev as she walked up. "Bev, tell these maniacs I'm not cheating! I grew these pumpkins from water and my own blend of fertilizer!"

"It's that fertilizer we want to see," Ollie said. "Bev, this isn't your concern."

Luckily, Herman *was* on the list of people Rustin had wanted her to talk with. "Oh, I'm helping Sheriff Rustin ask people about their magic." She showed them the list.

Casimir took it and frowned. "Why would he give this to you? It's supposed to be…" He let out a loud breath through his nose as he read through the list. "I don't believe Commander Mackey wanted this shared with the wider population of Pigsend."

"Oh, you know how small towns are," Bev said

nonchalantly. She hadn't even considered the implications for Rustin. "Word gets around. But you'll be pleased to note that I've already stopped in with a few of them. The Brewer twins were simply upset that Etheldra had fired Shasta—such a big blow for them, you know. Ramone is gone for the summer." She paused, getting an idea. "And so is Bathilda."

"How do you know that?" Ollie asked.

"They both had signs on their doors," Bev said, hoping they wouldn't double check her story. "In any case, Herman was the last person I was going to talk with today, and here you two are." She turned to Herman. "I doubt there's anything out of the ordinary here, right?"

"Not a *thing*," Herman said. "And if someone's out there spreading rumors that there is, it's probably that no-good Trent Scrawl. He's always had it out for me. Only won the Harvest Festival last year because my entry was destroyed by one of *you* confounded soldiers!"

"We're not trying to ruin anyone's…Harvest Festival?" Casimir said. "But you have to admit, these pumpkins are much larger than they should be."

"Look around," Bev said. "Everything in town is overflowing. The grass is practically up to my shoulders. The farmers' market can't sell their produce fast enough. If something's amiss, it's certainly not Herman's doing." Bev cleared her throat. "I'm actually walking the river looking for anything suspicious. Haven't seen anything yet."

"If there's anything suspicious around these parts, look no farther than Trent," Herman said with a loud huff. "Meanwhile, you three can get off my property so I can get back to tending to my crops."

~

The two soldiers, thankfully, took the hint and left with Bev. Without Zed or anyone to interrogate, Bev actually found their company quite nice. They chatted amiably about themselves, and where they were from. Ollie was from Sheepsburg, and had been in the queen's service throughout the war. Casimir was on the younger side and had joined right as the war began. The one thing they had in common was sharing Zed's passion for eradicating magical creatures.

"It's not fair," Ollie said. "We'd go into battle, and there would be hundreds of us on the queen's side up against one wizard, and we'd lose."

"Until Zed came along," Casimir said with a starry-eyed nod. "Then the tide turned, for sure. We're so grateful for his courage in coming to the right side."

Bev made a noncommittal noise. "He certainly risked a lot to do so, I hear."

"He can't go to certain parts of the country," Casimir said. "Otherwise, they'll run him out on a rail. Places like where Andres is from."

"Certainly, you might find your insurrectionists there," Bev said. "Instead of out in the rural countryside."

"This is the sort of place such a gathering would occur," Casimir said. "Precisely because it's quiet. You don't get soldiers like us here often."

That certainly hadn't been true of late. "Obviously, I don't remember things before the war, but when I talk with folks who've lived here their entire lives, they say not much changed for them after the war."

"Out here, sure," Ollie said. "But in the cities, where there was much more mingling of magical and not, things are so much better. Everyone's on even footing."

Casimir nodded emphatically. "That was the problem with magicals around every corner. You never knew what sort of tricks they had up their sleeves. You'd be walking down the street, and *poof,* you'd be turned into a newt."

"A newt?" Bev frowned. "Really?"

"Well, temporarily, maybe." He cleared his throat. "In any case, you don't have to worry about a wizard popping out of a bush or a demonic chicken attacking you or anything like that. Everyone's exactly who they say they are. No surprises."

Bev's leg scars could say otherwise about the

demonic chickens. "That's what I love about Pigsend, too. There's not a bad seed in the population. You've got a few grumps, a couple of folks who like to mind their own business. But for the most part, we all get along, and nobody makes waves."

They were almost back to town when Jemma, the third soldier, came running down the street, turning as soon as she saw her compatriots. The look on her face sent dread right into the bottom of Bev's stomach.

"What now?" she muttered.

"Ollie, Casimir," she said, breathlessly. "You have to come quickly. I don't know what happened, but—"

"What is it?" Ollie said, stepping forward.

She swallowed, looking at Bev, but perhaps decided time was of the essence. "I-it's our weapons."

"Are they missing?" Casimir asked, putting his hand on his sword. "Did someone attack the camp?"

Wordlessly, she pulled a large loaf of bread from behind her. It was a nice specimen, something that could've come from Bev's oven, if she shaped her loaves a little differently. But there was something about the shape of it—one long piece, with two smaller pieces coming off…like a sword and hilt.

"This is my sword," Jemma mumbled quietly.

"Are you joking?"

"I wish I were," Jemma said. "But…all the weapons we had in camp… They've all been turned into bread."

Chapter Seventeen

"Bread."

The soldiers had their compatriot repeat herself thrice before they finally accepted she wasn't talking nonsense and accompanied her back to the camp. While Bev had things to do back at the inn, her curiosity got the better of her, so she went with the two soldiers.

It seemed everyone else had been sent away on other tasks, and poor Jemma was the one left to guard things. By all accounts, it should've been simple. There wasn't a cloud in the blue sky, the sun was bright, and there weren't any trees, bushes, or anywhere to hide. If someone wanted to cause mischief, they'd be seen walking up to the camp.

Which, from the looks of things, was what had happened. Every one of their swords, knives, and spears were now beautifully baked loaves of bread. She picked up a round dinner-roll-looking item and hadn't a clue what that could've been.

"I swear, I was standing here, right in front of the tent," she said, her face pale and her voice shaking. "One minute, everything was fine. The next, I start smelling bread. Turn around, boom. It's all looking like…well, like this."

"And you didn't see anyone?" Casimir asked.

She shook her head. "No. I was patrolling the camp, as Zed told me to, and didn't take my eyes off the field—not even for an instant. I would've seen someone walking up, I swear it." She swallowed. "Whoever it was, they were able to cloak themselves and…well, do this."

"Dangerous." Casimir shook his head.

"Oh, come now," Bev said with a chuckle as she held the bread in her hands. "Turning weapons into bread? Seems like someone having a laugh, doesn't it? If they'd wanted to cause *real* harm, then…"

The look on their faces told Bev her platitudes were falling on deaf ears.

"Without our potions, we can't fix this," Ollie said, his expression grim. "So we're a cadre of soldiers in the middle of enemy territory without a single weapon. This is *very* serious."

"You aren't in enemy territory," Bev said.

"This is the third attack on our camp since we arrived," Casimir said. "Clearly, someone means us harm."

Bev couldn't argue with that, though she was still of the opinion that if someone wanted to harm them, they could do much more damage than simply turning their weapons to bread and transforming their horses.

"Oh, here he comes," Jemma said, looking past Bev's shoulder. "Now, I'm in for it."

Bev followed her gaze and spotted Zed walking up the road. "I doubt he can fault you for this," Bev said. "You were doing everything right. It's not—"

"Perhaps time for you to head back to the inn," Casimir said, swallowing hard. "This isn't going to be pretty."

~

Zed's red-faced berating of the three soldiers was the farthest cry from his easy-going demeanor at his son's wedding. Though Bev had taken the hint and left before he'd arrived, she'd stopped before town to watch them for a moment. But her own secondhand embarrassment soon got to be too much for her, and she turned and headed to town.

She could see why the soldiers, with their history of wars and enemies and horror, would see this latest incident as another shot across the bow. One intended to scare them into leaving or giving up or something along those lines. But the act itself was so…silly. Turning weapons into bread. The culprit could've chosen anything else—dust, water, flowers. But bread?

Someone seemed to be having a good time at the soldiers' expense.

Intent. Once again, that word came back to her mind. Percival had said very clearly that transforming one thing into something else was an advanced bit of magic. First the horses, now the weapons. What could be next? The soldiers themselves, turned into…what had he said? Newts?

Silly.

The whole thing was silly, in fact, but if Bev didn't figure out who was behind it, Zed would take his search to another level. She'd already seen a different side of him over the past few days, and she didn't want to see how far more hijinks would push him. She was also very grateful for her crumble, musing she should make more before Zed lined everyone up and pricked their fingers one by one.

It would be a fool's errand. She was *quite* sure that no one who lived in Pigsend had that kind of magic, which meant the troublemaker wasn't from Pigsend—and probably staying at her inn. Feliciano and Stephen, or Kemp. Or perhaps Andres—even though he'd supposedly been out and about with Vellora on meat deliveries. Biscuit hadn't come to get her yet, so she had to assume Solan was still in the inn.

Said laelaps was sleeping in the front room but awoke when Bev arrived. She watched him for a moment, considering her options.

"Would be nice if there were more of you," Bev muttered then thought better of it. "Never mind. I couldn't keep enough food in the inn."

Biscuit unfurled his tongue in a smile.

"I think we should adjust our focus," Bev said to Biscuit. "Do you think you can sniff out Feliciano or Stephen for me?"

He tilted his head, almost in question.

"Well, if Solan isn't leaving their room, you could find someone else, couldn't you?" Bev said.

"Does he answer?"

Bev nearly jumped out of her skin. Kemp stood in the doorway of the kitchen, munching on a piece of stale bread.

"I hope you don't mind," he said. "I was a bit hungry. Thought I'd help myself before dinner."

"Totally fine," Bev said. "And yes. I do talk to my dog. He's quite smart when he wants to be." She cleared her throat. "Can I help you with something?"

"No, passing through on my way back to my room," he said, lifting the small morsel of bread still in his hand. "Solan hasn't left yet, if you're wondering. I can hear them humming across the hall from me." He tapped his finger to his nose. "But I'll be sure to let you know if they do. I'm quite positive they're the one causing all this strangeness in town."

"You are?" Bev quirked a brow. "Why?"

"Just got a feeling." He nodded, as if he investigated these kinds of things on a regular basis. "Don't you worry, Ms. Bev, we'll figure this out together."

And with that, he all but jogged up the stairs.

"Hm." Bev shook her head before turning back to Biscuit. "What do you think? Care to find Feliciano and Stephen for me?"

Biscuit yawned and laid back down.

Bev frowned. "You don't think they're worth following, then?"

His only response was to start snoring.

Biscuit's opinions aside, Bev did have to get dinner going, so she vowed to question her guests when they came down to eat. Those plans, unfortunately, were completely upended when Zed and the soldiers walked through the door, looking like they'd packed up their camp. Zed must've decided the wide-open field was too dangerous. Jemma carried their weapons-turned-bread in a large bag on her back and kept her gaze on the ground. The other two also seemed unwilling to meet her gaze.

"Bev, do you have rooms to spare this evening?" Zed asked, and from his tone, Bev was sure if she *didn't*, he'd find some.

"We do, as a matter of fact," Bev said. "Two. Would you like to—"

"Yes." He put down the coins. "And I'd like to look at your list of who's staying at the inn this week."

"Sure." Bev slid the book over to him and pointed out the names. "Most have reserved their room through the solstice."

"I see." His finger lingered on Andres's name for longer than necessary. "Have you seen our mutual friend lately?"

"He's been going with Vellora, as I understand it," Bev said. "But I'm sure he'll be back for dinner." She paused, licking her lips and considering her words as she reached for the keys. "I'd like to ask that you remain civil when you're in the common areas. I do have a business to run, and—"

Zed glared at her, and she met his gaze unflinchingly.

"I understand you have bad blood, but I won't have my dining room turned into a free-for-all," Bev said, keeping a firm grip on the keys as she placed them on the counter. "Or else you and your soldiers will have to find another place to stay. Understand?"

She glanced around the room at the other three soldiers, but the only one who seemed hot under the collar was Zed.

After a too-long pause, he ground out, "Fine."

Bev released her grip, and he snatched the keys

immediately, turning to storm up the stairs with his soldiers in tow. Bev shook her head, wondering about the brilliance of having Andres and Zed staying under the same roof, but there was little she could do about it now. Still, the other man deserved to know, and Bev needed to pick up her meat, so after starting the ovens, she headed across the street to do both.

Ida was reading a book at the front counter and brightened when Bev walked in. "Hi, Bev! I've got your order ready for you."

"Wonderful," Bev said. "How are you feeling?"

"All right," Ida said. "This morning, Lillie brought by a cup of tea she said was brewed in iron. Tasted awful but had the desired effect." She made a face. "I hope Zed plans on moving on soon. I'm quite sick of him, you know?"

"Unfortunately, I come bearing bad news," Bev said with a shake of her head. "I wanted to let Andres know Zed has...erm...invited himself to stay at the inn."

Ida gave Bev a sideways look. "And you let him?"

"Ida, you know I have to accept everyone who comes through my door," Bev said. "And I told him to be on his best behavior where Andres is concerned. Besides, he already tested you two and didn't find anything. So you shouldn't see any more of him."

"Unless he wants to come and watch Andres all day," Ida said. "Which I'm sure is next."

Bev couldn't argue with that. "Is Andres intent on staying until the solstice? Not that I want to kick Vellora's old commander out of town, but it would ease some of the tension if he headed back home."

"I said the same to Vellora," Ida said. "She was adamant that he stay. In her mind, why should *he* have to go when *Zed* is the one here unplanned." She shook her head. "I swear, I love my wife, but she can be so pigheaded sometimes."

"At least she's keeping him out of town," Bev said. "Small blessing there."

Ida nodded, but she looked a little uneasy. "Don't… Well, I know you won't mention this to Zed. But we've never had so many meat deliveries. Half the time, Vellora's leaving and coming back with an empty wagon."

"What do you think they're doing?" Bev asked.

"I don't know. Vel could be keeping him out of town so he's got an alibi." She nodded, as if convincing herself. "Yes, I'm sure that's what it is."

"The soldiers' weapons were turned into bread today," Bev said. "Between that and their horses into caterpillars, it seems…"

"Childish?" Ida offered. "Who turns swords into bread other than someone looking to have a good laugh?"

"Exactly. But I also can see why Zed's

concerned. They don't have weapons—"

"Not that they need any," Ida said, her eyes sharpening. "There aren't any battles to fight in Pigsend. And if there are, they're starting them."

"Now you sound like your wife," Bev said with a smile.

Ida's face reddened. "Well, they seem to be the ones causing all the problems they claim to be here to fix."

"I don't know. Those globes last night were something else," Bev said. She snapped her fingers. "I should probably tell Max that Zed will be at dinner, too. He was a bit too vocal last night, and I don't think he's going to want to break bread with him."

"Probably not," Ida said. "I know I wouldn't. Glad I'm not in a business where I have to cater to them."

Bev didn't have the heart to remind her that the meat she sold to Bev would be going straight into the bellies of said soldiers and just asked if it was ready.

~

Bev stopped at the inn long enough to get the meat prepped and in the oven then was glad for a reason to leave the sweltering kitchen. She walked briskly down the street, mentally calculating how long the chicken needed to cook and how much time she had to chitchat with Max.

The clock on the town hall said it was nearing four, which meant the library would close soon. But Max was still behind the counter, dusting and rearranging things as he moved from shelf to shelf.

The poor man nearly jumped out of his skin when the door opened. He spun then visibly relaxed. "Oh, it's you, Bev."

"Expecting someone else?" Bev asked with a curious look.

"Well, you know, after my outburst last night," Max said, his cheeks red—though that might've been from the heat. "Zed came in and read me the riot act. Pricked my finger and everything. But I seemed to pass his test, for the moment."

Bev nodded. "He's decided to stay at the inn instead of a camp outside town. In case you were planning on coming to dinner."

He shook his head. "I wasn't planning on it, no. Too dangerous even to leave the library until everything blows over." He paused. "Has something else happened? I saw they caught all the runaway magic."

Bev told him about the bread weapons, and he let out a low whistle. "Someone's keen on causing trouble."

"Any idea who it could be?" Bev asked. "I don't think there's anyone in town with that kind of power, do you? So it has to be someone at the inn."

"The problem, Bev, is that with the increased

magic from the river, all bets are off in terms of who's got what powers," Max said. "Someone who didn't have magic before might have something awakened in them."

Bev nodded, thinking of Allen's newfound magic. "But Perc… A friend who knows a lot about magic told me that transforming one thing into something else takes a great deal of skill. I doubt someone who's just come into their magic would be able to do that."

"True," Max said.

Bev hesitated, not wanting to press but needing to know. "Your friends, Stephen and Feliciano—"

"Not my friends." It came out a little too quickly and forcefully.

"Well, you've been taking walks with them," Bev said, holding up her hands in surrender. "Could they be involved in any way? I'm not going to tell Zed, but if they are, then—"

"I don't know," he said with a sigh. "Their political affiliations aside, I don't think there's anything worth mentioning about them. They don't have any sort of magic I can sense, in any case. And they don't seem like the people who'd want to cause trouble."

"That's it. None of it seems to make sense," Bev said. "It doesn't seem calculated. Random, almost."

"Disarming the soldiers, even in a childish way, is still disarming them," Max said. "Whoever's responsible may have a funny way of going about it, but their ends are deadly serious."

Chapter Eighteen

Bev wasn't looking forward to dinner. She hid in the kitchen, despite the heat, if only to delay the inevitable tension-filled evening as long as possible. But as the front room clock chimed, she could avoid it no longer, and plastered a smile on her sweat-covered face as she brought out the plate of dinner.

As feared, she was the only one smiling.

Zed and his three soldiers sat at one table, each one stormy-faced, but none so much as Zed. The subject of his ire sat on the other side of the room, glaring back at him.

Joining Andres at his table were Feliciano and Stephen, nervously twitching as they fiddled with their hands, and Kemp, whose gaze was on the staircase. He tapped his nose and nodded at Bev, as if they were in on something together, then returned to his surveillance.

At the middle table, Etheldra and Earl waited for their meal, looking like they regretted coming to the Weary Dragon this evening. Earl gave Bev a sideways look and Etheldra had her arms crossed over her chest, as if everyone in the room was offensive to her.

"Erm," Bev said, after a long pause. "Dinner is served."

No one moved for a moment. Then Etheldra rose, followed by Earl, Kemp, Feliciano, and Stephen. Zed's soldiers stood next, with a cautious look at their commander, who was still glaring at his nemesis. But Andres didn't stand until everyone (save Zed) had served themselves and was digging into their meal. He stood, stretching as if there wasn't a glare on him, and leisurely crossed the room to pick up a plate.

"Looks delicious," he said to Bev.

"I hope that Ida told you…" Bev cleared her throat, her gaze drifting over to Zed.

"She did. Thank you for that," Andres said, his smile calm and unbothered. "I hope our combined presence doesn't cause you any undue stress, Ms. Bev. You've been so hospitable."

"As long as everyone behaves themselves," she said. "I already gave Zed a speech about remaining civil, but—"

"Believe me, I have no interest in attracting attention," he said, adding a chicken leg to his plate. "I'm here visiting a friend, and nothing more."

Something about his denial made her suspicious. Ida had, of course, planted the seed in her ear by saying Andres and Vellora had been coming and going with an empty wagon. But his complete lack of nerves paradoxically made him look more guilty. Once again, Bev questioned what could be so important that he'd want to stay in town. Surely, catching up with Vellora didn't merit all this.

After he served himself, Bev looked at Zed and waited, but he kept his unflinching gaze on Andres. The room was silent, except for silverware scraping against the wooden bowls. Finally, Bev tired of his scrutiny, so she made him a plate and walked across the room to deliver it.

"Remember what I said," Bev said, placing the meal in front of Zed.

"I haven't said a word," Zed said, his attention shifting away from Andres to Bev. "And I'm not hungry."

"It'll go bad," Bev said, pushing the plate closer. "Eat. You'll feel better."

"I'll feel better when I catch the person attacking me and my soldiers," Zed said, glaring at Andres.

"He wasn't in town all day," Bev said, waving her hand in front of Zed's face. "He was out with

Vellora. As I'm sure you already know."

He sniffed and picked up his fork. "I hear Rustin asked you to walk around town asking questions for him. I'll have to have a chat with him about the nature of his duties, and when to delegate them. You aren't a member of the queen's service, and I'm *not* exactly sure what you're up to—"

"Trying to help," Bev said, reaching into her pocket to pull out the piece of paper Rustin had given her earlier in the day. "In any case, I spoke to everyone on the list. Nothing strange to report."

"Is that so?" Zed pulled the paper over to him. "Ollie, Casimir, you went to speak with Herman Monday about those gigantic pumpkins?"

"He says they're normal," Casimir said.

"They *are* normal," Bev said then added, "As normal as everything is right now."

"And those twins who seem to be telepathic?" Zed asked.

"Just dealing with some stress from one of them losing their job," Bev said, crossing her arms. "But Etheldra came by and all is well. Shasta will be back at work tomorrow, won't she?"

Etheldra glared at Bev but nodded.

"Bathilda?"

"Out of town."

"That's funny, because she practically ran me off her property the other day," Zed said, eyeing her.

"Well, perhaps gone for the week, then. I hear

there are some strange people in town who might've spooked her." Bev spoke with a smile, but internally, she was worried. What if Zed went to Bathilda again? She definitely couldn't hide that phoenix. "In any case, nobody in town is capable of the sort of magic that keeps afflicting you, so—"

"Which is why we're staying near to the *new elements* in town," Zed said with a knowing smile. He cleared his voice and rose. "Everyone who isn't a Pigsend resident, please stay in the dining room after dinner so we can ask you a few questions."

"Are we under arrest?" Feliciano asked. "And if so, for what crime?"

"No one is under arrest, for the moment," Zed said, scanning the room. "But we'd like to know where you were today. And please," he smiled humorlessly, "let us know if you have witnesses to your stories."

"Well, I was at the inn all day," Kemp announced loudly. "But the person staying in the room next to mine, they're the one you should be looking into."

Zed turned to Kemp with a raised eyebrow. "Why? Did they leave their room?"

"Erm, no. But I get a funny feeling about them." He shifted. "They showed up looking like a witch, and—"

"If they didn't leave the inn today, I don't care." Zed waved him off. "And do *you* have a list of witnesses who saw you here?"

Kemp turned to Bev, pleading in his gaze. She took pity on the poor man, though she figured she'd have to tell him to leave Solan alone. Being a little strange wasn't a crime. "I saw him here."

"You weren't at the inn all day," Zed said. "As you said, you were crisscrossing the town doing Rustin's job."

Bev closed her mouth. He did have her there.

"There was no one else," Kemp said, his face reddening.

"Then we should go upstairs and check with Solan." Zed rose. "The rest of you, stay here and answer my soldiers' questions. Kemp, why don't you come upstairs with me?"

"I'll come, too," Bev said. "It is my inn, after all."

~

Kemp, of course, was much less confident as he led the group up the stairs. Zed didn't seem to recognize the other man, so Bev's initial suspicions that the man was a soldier in disguise were starting to fade.

"I swear, I was here all day," Kemp said, wringing his hands as they walked down the hall.

"And why *are* you in town?" Zed asked, scrutinizing him.

Kemp shared a nervous look with Bev. "I'm… here on official business, actually. I don't particularly want it shared, in case, but—"

"In case what?" Bev asked.

"My work is secretive," he said.

Zed made a noise, and to Bev's surprise, didn't inquire further. "Where is this Solan staying?"

"Right here." Bev rapped on Solan's door and waited.

They opened the door with a flourish. "Good evening. Can I help you?"

Bev peered past them, a little shocked at the transformation of the room behind them. They'd draped thick purple curtains across all the windows (oh, the nail holes!), they'd hung a twinkling chandelier with a single burning candle from the ceiling, and moved the bed across the room. Everything smelled of some herb Bev couldn't place, too. She could only imagine how long it would take her to air it out.

"Yes," Zed said slowly as he took in the sight, too. "I wanted to ask where you were today."

"Right here." They leaned against the door. "It's the solstice. Far too much chaos out there for me to feel safe leaving my room."

"Why do you say that?" Zed said.

"Silly man," Solan said. "It's the solstice, as I said."

Zed waited, presumably waiting for Solan to expand upon that, but they simply shrugged and gestured to Kemp. "This lovely man was in the room next to me all day. I heard him talking to himself." They beamed at Kemp. "Surely, he can vouch for me."

Kemp's face went red, and he stammered something about hearing Solan.

"Well, there you have it," Solan said to Zed. "Now if you'll excuse me, I've got to keep this door closed. The incense will dilute if too much leaves the room."

"What's the—" Zed began, but the door slammed in his face. He seemed torn between demanding Solan open it again and turning to leave.

"I think that about covers it," Bev said lightly. "Solan and Kemp were here all day. Seems we can strike them off our list of suspects, hm?"

Zed glared at her before turning to storm downstairs.

"As for you," Bev said to Kemp with a look, "maybe this will teach you to stop judging people for being a little different. Solan isn't bothering you. And—"

"But they *weren't here* all day," Kemp whispered, eyes wide with fear. "I swear, I saw them walking down the street earlier. But the incessant humming in their room didn't end. *Something* strange is going on with them." He swallowed, glancing after Zed. "Maybe I should—"

"Maybe you should be grateful that Solan vouched for you," Bev said. "Because otherwise, you might find yourself in trouble."

He closed his mouth and nodded.

"Now, go get some rest. Clearly, the heat's getting to you if you're imagining things," Bev said. "And I'd better not hear a peep out of you about your neighbor. Understand?"

~

As Bev returned downstairs, she was met with silence. Feliciano and Stephen sat where they'd been, their arms folded across their chests. Andres seemed the least annoyed of the bunch, perhaps because he'd been under almost constant scrutiny since he'd arrived.

"What's your business in town?" Zed asked the two men.

"Ours," Stephen said.

"Is it a crime to travel the country?" Feliciano asked.

"No, but it is a crime to steal from a member of the queen's service," Zed said. "If I go upstairs, will I find my chest of potions in your room?"

"If they stole such a thing, do you think they'd be so foolish as to leave it in their possession?" Andres asked. "Really, Zed, use some logic."

"You keep quiet," Zed barked. "You'll get your turn later."

"You know my business," Andres said. "I'm here visiting my dear friend Vellora. I plan to stay until the day after the solstice." He bowed. "If that will be all, it *has* been a long day. I'm going to retire." He paused at the bottom of the stairs. "You've already searched my rooms, so please forgive me if I don't want you to search them again."

Zed glowered but didn't stop him, instead turning his ire onto Feliciano and Stephen. "As I was saying…what's your business in town?"

Bev took the opportunity to disappear into the kitchen, as she didn't much care *what* their business was, and she had a mountain of dishes. She kept the door propped open, but there was very little to hear. As nerve-wracking as being questioned seemed, there really wasn't much to it. Stephen and Feliciano didn't have witnesses for their stories, as they'd been walking the farmlands in search of fresh air, they said. They hadn't a clue about bread weapons, and if they found it funny, they had enough sense to keep that to themselves. They had their fingers pricked and came back clean, but Zed still searched their rooms. He presumably found nothing, because he didn't return downstairs.

"Just a few days until the solstice," Bev muttered to herself. "A few days and all this mess will be over with."

She jumped as a wet nose pressed against her leg.

"Oh, it's you, Biscuit," she said. "Did I forget to feed you?"

He unfurled his tongue and wagged his tail.

"What is it?" Bev said.

Biscuit growled, and his golden eyes darted toward the door.

"No, Solan is upstairs," Bev said, lowering her voice. "Right? Or is there something else I need to see?"

Biscuit padded toward the back door.

"Well, I trust you," Bev muttered, taking off her apron and following.

~

Biscuit jogged at a good clip, and Bev hurried to keep up. The air was thick with moisture and something else, and Bev felt funny being out in it. Like she should turn around and go back to the inn. But Biscuit kept a steady pace, and the laelaps had never steered her wrong before.

"The dark forest?" Just as Kemp had said. Score one for the nosy man.

As she approached, she slowed, not sure what she might find. In the past, she'd found both Allan and later, his wedding planner in the dark forest, bartering with the barus, a magical creature who could create magical baubles to give the bearer the abilities of other magic users, like pobyds and leprechauns. Another time, she'd witnessed Dag Flanigan arresting someone for selling a wyvern egg. Suffice to say, it wasn't her favorite place in Pigsend. But it was a great place to practice magic, if one were looking to do that.

Biscuit's nose pressed to the ground, and his white-tipped tail bounced through the underbrush. The forest itself was sentient, and it let both her and Biscuit through without a fight. Everything was quiet, and seemed almost unchanged, except for those curious orange vines. They'd sprouted leaves and buds now, and shuddered as Bev walked by.

In a clearing, Bev spotted a figure walking in a circle, humming to themselves.

Solan.

But how could that be? There was one staircase in the inn, and Bev had literally just seen them in their room.

Bev crouched low as she moved closer, confused. Solan finally stopped, crossing their legs as they sat on the ground. They pressed their hands together in prayer for a long, silent moment. Then they raised them to the air.

"Oh, Mother Earth, why are you so unsettled? Please, allow me to help."

They pressed their palms to the ground. The dark forest shifted around Bev, and bright lights shimmered in the dirt right beneath their hands. They dug their fingers deeper into the dirt, and more lights danced along the ground.

When they opened their eyes, they were *glowing* —almost like those floating orbs. *Magic.* Magic in its purest form.

"I know you're there, Ms. Bev," Solan said,

though they didn't sound cross about it. "Please come out if you're going to watch. It's disrupting my concentration to have you lurk."

Bev jumped, looking around. She was well hidden, so how——?

"The forest told me you're here," Solan said with a kind smile. "Really, come on out. I have precious little time to work, and I can't afford to dillydally."

Bev cleared her throat and stepped out. "And what, exactly, are you doing? You aren't the cause of all this excess magic, are you?"

They laughed, and the sound was high and melodious. "Goodness, *no*. I'm trying to *help*." They beckoned her forward. "I can only do so much, but I'm trying to siphon off as much as I can to alleviate some of the pressure."

"Siphon the magic?" Bev asked. "So you can wield it?"

"Of course!" They didn't seem put out by the admission. "After all, I am a witch."

Chapter Nineteen

Bev had heard of witches mentioned in passing but had no context for them. Solan spoke as if it were common knowledge; then again, Solan didn't seem the type to think anything was strange.

"Is that like a wizard?" Bev asked.

"Oh, no, no. They've got much more capacity for magic," they said, once again digging their hands into the ground. "Wizards can cast and conjure and transfigure with the use of a wand or staff. Witches are more in tune with the earth and the mundane, which we use to wield our magic. If the earth allows it, we can do great things. But if it doesn't..." They chuckled, rubbing their hands together. "The earth can be a fickle thing."

"How did you get out of the inn?" Bev asked,

"Hm?"

"Just now," Bev said. "I was in the kitchen. I would've seen you leave—"

"Ah. I haven't been at the inn all day."

"But I saw you!" Bev gestured toward Pigsend. "And Kemp said you were humming in your room. And I'd set Biscuit to keep watch on you and let me know if you left."

"Ah, your laelaps!" They laughed. "That explains his interest in me, then. I thought it might be because of the magic. I came down a few times, and he popped up ready to follow me. So I cast a spectral projection of myself. Departed early this morning before anyone was awake."

"What, exactly, is that?" Bev said.

"It's a vision of myself that I left in the room," Solan said. "If you'd reached out and touched me, your hand would've gone right through me. Good thing you didn't! Might've given that soldier a fright."

And he would've arrested you.

Solan simply smiled. "And what are you doing in this dark, sentient forest on this pleasant evening?"

Bev's face flushed. "Well… looking for you, actually."

"Oh? Why?"

"Trying to figure out what in the world is going

on with the river," Bev said. "Because I don't think this amount of magic is normal—even for a full moon at solstice. And the soldiers at the inn are bound and determined to find someone to blame their misfortunes on."

"Well, you're right about one thing: this amount of magic *isn't* normal," Solan said, gazing at the ground with concern. "Something else is enhancing the magic. I can't put my finger on exactly what—or for what purpose."

"I have some theories about that," Bev said. "I think someone's tampering with the river to hide themselves. And I have a hunch it's the same person who's messing with the soldiers."

"Messing with the soldiers?" Solan chuckled. "The soldiers are busy enough chasing their own tails. They don't need someone playing practical jokes on them."

"They don't seem to think it's funny," Bev said. "And they're about ready to burn the village down looking for the culprit."

"Well, it's not me," Solan said. "I don't have a great deal of magic, nor do I have any desire to disrupt this beautiful land and the lush power running beneath it."

Bev watched them as they ran their fingers along the dirt. "Then what are you doing, exactly?"

"As I said, absorbing some of it," Solan said. "To alleviate the pressure. But goodness, there's so much more magic than I can digest. Even now, I'll have to spend the evening in the forest so I don't leave a trail behind me and alert those curious soldiers."

"Do you think a fellow witch might be... I don't know, increasing the power of the river so they can absorb more?" Bev asked.

"To what end?" Solan tilted their head.

Bev could think of several reasons a creature might want more power, especially with all the talk of a rebellion going on. Was it all connected? Were there a cadre of magical creatures eager to absorb power so they might bring war, ruin, and more horrible things back to this land?

Bev clicked her tongue. This was getting too political for her. "Are you the only kind of creature who can absorb magic like this?"

"Everyone can absorb magic, in some way or another. Even wizards, who have more magic than they know what to do with, can always take a little more." They sat back, looking up at the sky, which had almost taken on a purple hue. "It's going to be a rough night, though."

"Why?"

"There's lots of magic in the air. Too much to be stable." They sighed, rising and dusting off their hands. "A magical storm is brewing. Might be best for you to get back to the inn where it's safe."

"What's a magical storm?" Bev asked. "Is that like a thunderstorm, or...?"

"Similar concept, but the outcome is much different. A magical storm is unpredictable. It can transfigure anything into anything. No rhyme or reason. They're very rare events, of course." They shook their head. "Best to stay indoors tonight."

"And you?"

"I should be safe here in the forest," they said. "Nobody will be bothering me tonight."

"What if Zed comes to search your room again?" Bev asked. "How long does this…projection last?"

"Zed wouldn't dare set foot inside my room," Solan said with a chuckle. "The first time I saw him at the inn, I started burning a little bit of basil with the incense."

Basil. "That's what I was smelling."

"It's good for keeping out pests. And in this case, a soldier is *definitely* a pest. But it's such a mild suggestion that he'll never know he was spelled. Just that he doesn't want to enter my room for his own unexplained reasons."

That seemed dangerous, but she got the distinct impression Solan never worried about anything.

There was an ominous rumbling in the distance, and Solan frowned. "Best hop to it, Ms. Bev. Don't want to be walking around when this storm hits."

~

Bev left Solan in the forest, amazed at how little they seemed to care for their own safety. Sleeping in the open in the dark forest? Leaving spells and magic in their room? Everyone else in town was desperate to hide their magic from prying eyes, but Solan simply made them turn the other way.

As soon as she left the dark forest, the magic in the air increased. The atmosphere seemed thick with something, as if a rainstorm was about to unleash from above, but there wasn't a cloud in the sky. It made the hair on Bev's arms stand up. Though the temperature was warm, a chill ran down her spine. Whether it was her own worry about the solstice's apex tomorrow, Solan's warning about the impending magical storm, or something else, she didn't know.

Once again, more questions, few answers. Solan, presumably, was off her list of suspects. But what about Andres? What about Feliciano and Stephen? Even Kemp, with his nervous twitching, was clearly hiding something.

But she hadn't even closed the door behind her when a voice called out, "Where were you?"

Zed sat at the kitchen table, his feet stretched out beneath him and hands clasped behind his head.

"Out for a walk," Bev said. "Biscuit, erm… Biscuit got out. Caught the scent of a rabbit, I think. And once he gets an idea in his head, it's downright impossible to get him to heel, unless you can catch him. Took me all this time to get him."

"He's lucky to have you as an owner, then," Zed

said. From the tone, Bev wasn't sure if he believed her.

Bev had never considered herself his *owner*, more like his food source and warm-bed provider. "Did you talk with everyone? Any new suspects?"

"Yes." He tilted his head up. "You."

"Me?" Bev laughed. "Zed, come now. Why would I have any cause to bother you? In fact, I'm trying to help figure out who it is."

"And why, Bev, are you doing that?" Zed asked. "Why are you always the one who ends up in the middle of these things?"

"I don't know, honestly, and I often wish Rustin or someone else would handle it instead," Bev said. "But at the end of the day, it's usually me."

"Rustin told me you *insisted* on helping," Zed said. "Took the list from him. Then I hear you've been passing out your crumble to everyone."

Bev lifted a shoulder, trying to look neutral. "As I said, the farmers had plenty of produce. I couldn't possibly use them all for dinner, so I thought I'd make something sweet and share it with the town."

"Even with Allen next door baking his tail off?" He nodded to the edge of the table where Bev's crumble pan sat. "Curious that you baked it with willow bark," he said, leveling his gaze at her. "That's an interesting aromatic. And I found the satchel with iron nails in it, too."

"Are you getting at something, Zed?" Bev asked

with a sigh. "Because it has been a *very* long day."

"Did you find anything amiss with the river?" Zed asked. "Or were you too busy serving the magical folk of Pigsend iron-and-willow-laced rhubarb crumble?"

"The only thing amiss is that it's high," Bev said. "And as for the crumble, the willow bark was to aid the aches and pains. Clearly some kind of flu going around town, with half the folks laid up in bed with headaches."

"Conveniently, all those folks were also on my list," Zed said. "And conveniently fully on the mend once they had some of your dessert."

Bev put her hands on her hips. She really was tired of beating around the bush. So she waited for him to continue.

He rose and pulled his wrap of magical testing pins from the back pocket. "To be honest, I didn't want to test you because I didn't want to know. You've been such a good friend to my son, and you were instrumental in figuring out who was trying to ruin their wedding. I heard through the grapevine that your arrival was suspicious, and Dag Flanigan is convinced you're a member of the King's Wizard Corps, maybe even one of the Quartet. I don't think it's a coincidence that Andres is here, either."

"He's here to visit—"

"Vellora Witzel, who is known to have kingside sympathies," Zed said. "Bev, you have to see how all this is adding up."

"Except the part where I'm involved," Bev said. "As you said at the wedding: who I was before Pigsend doesn't matter. I'm not consorting with magical people, other than to figure out who might be targeting you."

"To help me or help them?" Zed asked.

Bev hadn't been expecting that question and took too long to answer. "You, obviously."

He gave her a sideways look as he approached. "Give me your finger."

She held out her hand, heart beating wildly, and found herself almost…excited. Was she finally going to learn the truth about herself?

Before he could prick her finger, the door burst open, and Casimir came running inside. "Commander! Come quick! You have to see this!"

Bev and Zed shared a look then scrambled to the front of the inn, where Ollie and Jemma were waiting. Bev held her breath, scanning the sky and town for what could've caused Casimir to come running. There didn't seem to be anything amiss, save the thick air and the nearly-full moon casting a bright glow across the quiet town.

At least, until an ominous rumbling echoed from somewhere in the sky.

Zed's gaze swept upward, as if looking for something. And if the fear on his face was any indication, that something wasn't good.

"What's happening?" Bev asked Zed.

"Magic storm," he said with a scowl.

Bev swallowed, hoping her face looked passive. "What's that?"

"When too much magic is concentrated in a single area, it makes for a bad time," Zed said. "The magical orbs were the first sign that things were too bad. Now we're really in trouble."

A bolt of purple lightning illuminated the sky, leaving behind a streak of what could only be described as stardust. She couldn't see where it had come from, but soon enough there was another. And the sky, which was inky black, began to glow an incandescent green as if reflecting a bright river.

Biscuit barked loudly as another light split the sky, and Bev decided she didn't want her laelaps getting in trouble. "Go back inside, Biscuit," she said, opening the door to the inn. "It's too dangerous for you out here."

The laelaps whined, but complied, and Bev heaved a sigh of relief as soon as his tail disappeared through the opening.

"We've got to evacuate the town," Zed said to the three soldiers.

"Evacuate?" Bev said. "Surely, people can shelter in place?"

Another purple streak passed—too close this time, slamming into a flowerpot in front of the butcher shop. It transformed into a bubbling cauldron, spitting steam and sparks.

Bev gasped, covering her mouth.

"*That* is why we have to evacuate the town," Zed said. "Magic storms are unpredictable. You'll be in your living room, and a bolt of magic will turn you *and* your house into something else." He put his hands to his head, staring at the bubbling cauldron. "And I don't have my potions to undo anything, either. So we'd better hope it doesn't hit anyone—"

Another stream came down and zapped Jemma right in the back. Her scream echoed for a moment, but then all that was left in her place was a small tree with golden-colored leaves that were eerily similar to her hair.

Bev jumped back in fear, and Zed cursed as he strode forward. "See what I mean?"

"S-surely, you'll be able to change her back," Bev said, unable to tear her gaze away from the tree.

"If I can get some potions, yes, but for now, she's safer like that," Zed said. "She's not going to be the last thing to transform, mark my words."

"How do we stop it?" Bev asked.

"We don't," he said grimly. "It's too powerful for any one person to stop. And *this* is why magic needs to be outlawed, Bev. Whatever you're hiding, whoever you're hiding, they caused this. They're going to be responsible for all the damage in town. So whatever you know, you need to *tell me*."

Bev stared at him. She really didn't know

anything. Solan was currently in the dark forest, trying to absorb the magic as fast as they could. The other magical folk in town were suffering from the increased magic as much as anyone else. There wasn't a single person she could pin this on or a motive she could definitively point to.

Zed let out a breath at her silence and threw his hands in the air. "Impossible. You're keen to feed everyone in town iron to hide their magic, but—"

"Wait, that's it," Bev said with a gasp. "Iron."

"Yes, iron will stop magic's effects," Zed said, impatiently.

"No. I mean, yes, but…" She took a moment to measure her thoughts. "What if we took whatever the blacksmith has in his shop and buried it around town?"

"What?" Zed frowned. "What would that do?"

"Karolina had a large iron contraption that helped stop the flow of magic," Bev said. "The river was stopped completely—that's what caused the sinkholes. If we buried iron in the ground where we know the river is highest, maybe—"

He nodded slowly. "It could work. If you know exactly where the river crests."

Chapter Twenty

Bev did know where the river was highest, so she led the three soldiers through town to Gore's shop. The blacksmith wasn't there, which meant Zed had to kick down the door to get inside. The soldiers grabbed whatever they could—scythes, nails, hammers, wheel parts—then turned to Bev for directions. She sent Ollie up to Herman's farm, telling him to bury the iron near his large pumpkins. Casimir was sent to Rosie's backyard. Bev and Zed carried armfuls of iron wheel parts to the inn, where Bev used the edge of the iron to dig a hole where the sinkhole had been all those months ago.

"I don't think this is going to work, Bev," Zed

said, looking up at the sky, which was even more alive than it had been. "We have to find out what's causing the magic to spike."

"What's going on?" Allen called from across the street. He and Lillie stood at the threshold of the bakery, watching the sky with trepidation. Next door, Ida was lingering in her doorway. Andres and Vellora were nowhere to be seen, but Bev didn't want to think about that right now. Not when the town was in danger of turning into—

Another flash of light, and the pretty awning over the bakery turned into icing, which landed with a *splat* on the street.

Lillie yelped and jumped backward, and Allen covered his head.

"Get back inside," Zed barked at him. "Or better yet, go hide in a root cellar. You don't want to be outside during—"

Cluck.

All heads turned toward the east, where a large, shadowy figure stood. If Bev hadn't known Pigsend inside and out, she would've sworn it was another building, but no. This was new.

Cluck.

A flash of light split the sky, illuminating what was a *very* large chicken with a pouf on its head. It strutted forward, scratching and picking at the ground as if it were perfectly normal for chickens the size of houses to walk down the street.

"What in the…?" Allen said, the color draining from his face. "Is that one of Rosie's chickens?"

"Goodness, I hope not," Bev muttered, taking a step back. "Don't tell me that thing was hit by a lightning bolt."

"No, that looks like it absorbed too much magic," Zed said. "They were already larger than they should've been. If I had my potions—"

"Well, you don't," Bev snapped. "So what's next?"

"Bev!" Shasta was running down the street wearing her dressing gown, her face pale with fright. "Bev, come quick!"

"What now?" Zed muttered.

They were able to sidestep the chicken by sliding through the houses and going north one street, then followed Shasta. The twins' house, which Earl had so painstakingly rebuilt after it had fallen into a sinkhole, was now dangling precipitously on the limb of a gigantic vine. Said vine, which looked eerily similar to the plants Bev had seen growing in pots in the Brewer house, was reaching toward the purple-tinted sky.

Stella stood beside her sister, in an identical dressing gown, with her hands over her mouth as she watched their house far above their heads.

"What do we—"

A large fireball split the sky. No, not a fireball— a fire*bird*. Bathilda's phoenix soared through the air, red and gold feathers ablaze as it circled the vine, the town hall building, everywhere it could. Bev winced as the burning tail feathers nearly caught the clock.

"Okay, since when has Pigsend had *phoenixes*?" Zed said, putting his hand to his head.

As if on cue, Bathilda came sprinting up the road, her hair smoking and her apron half-burned off. She took one look at Zed and seemed to regret leaving her house.

"Watch out!" Bev cried.

The phoenix let out that familiar squawk of distress, but this time, as it exploded, it lit up the entire night sky like Earl's fireworks show. Burning embers rained down on the town, catching some of the dry roofs.

"Oh, no!" Bev cried. The last thing they needed was the town burning down on top of everything else.

"Go get water buckets," Earl called, appearing with Etheldra. "We've got to get this fire out before it spreads!"

They got to work, gathering more people from the safety of their houses to rush down to Pigsend Creek. Bev didn't love the idea of everyone out and about, especially with the lightning strikes as they were. But if they didn't move, the whole town could burn down.

"The iron in the ground doesn't seem to be helping," Zed said, turning to Bev. "Clearly, we need to try something else."

Another split of purple sped across the sky, this time hitting the top of the vine holding the twins' house. At once, the vine went from a vibrant green to an even more vibrant yellow and orange—and the home was transformed into a large orange flower, reminding Bev of the vines currently growing in the dark forest.

"Maybe it's not the what, but the where," Bev said. "That contraption Karolina put in the ground was near the forest on the north side of town. If we bury iron there, maybe that will slow the storm down."

Zed winced—another bolt, and a nearby horse was turned into a stuffed animal. "We may want to consider that the time for stopping the storm is over and evacuate Pigsend."

Bev considered his words, but only for a moment. "If everyone leaves their homes, will they be safer? Or would they run the risk of being zapped by one of these lightning bolts?"

Zed didn't seem to have an answer he liked. "To the dark forest, then."

~

They stopped by the blacksmith's shop again to grab more things to bury then rushed down the road toward the dark forest. Bev hoped with every fiber of her being that Solan had left—or were at least far enough inside that they wouldn't be seen.

Zed wouldn't hesitate to blame a witch, even if said witch was trying to help.

At this time of night, the forest should've blended into the dark landscape, but the combination of bright moon overhead and dazzling magical lights gave them a clear view of it—and of the chaos the storm was wreaking out here.

Herman's pumpkins were the size of carriages now, and the grass along the side of the road had grown almost as tall as the trees. Everywhere Bev looked, there were signs that the magic was out of control—including a collection of magical balls floating by.

"I sure hope this works," Zed muttered. "Because if not, we've still got to get through the *actual* solstice tomorrow."

Bev didn't want to think about it but had hope that this harebrained scheme would work. The dark forest was up ahead, and she knew approximately where Karolina had planted the large iron thing.

But before they could turn off the main road, a crack of thunder echoed loudly around them, and a bolt of magic flew through Zed. His eyes bulged as his body collapsed in on itself, until a small object dropped onto the dirt road.

"Zed!" Bev cried, rushing toward him. As she knelt, her eyes swept over his new form.

A gingerbread man—complete with a little iced angry frown.

"We'll set you right. I promise," Bev whispered, picking up the small cookie and tucking it inside her shirt.

The magical bolts were increasing in frequency, lighting up the sky every few moments, so Bev walked carefully toward the dark forest, conscious of the cookie in her shirt. If any part of it crumbled, so, presumably, would Zed.

As she approached the forest, her hopes began to fade. She could feel the magic pulsing in the air, and the forest, which had been overwhelming before, was now almost too much to bear. The small scythe she carried, even made of iron, wouldn't do anything to stop the tide. She wasn't completely helpless—she might be able to call in a favor from Percival—but somehow she thought this chaos might be too much for the wizard.

"Bev?"

She looked up sharply at the sound of her name.

"Bev! Get in here!" Vellora stood at the edge of the forest, worry plain on her face. "Come, come! Before you get hit by this magic!"

Bev ran over, somewhat grateful to have eyes on the butcher. "What are you doing out here? And where have you been? The town is going nuts!"

"What are you talking about?" Andres said. "Is it Zed?"

"It's not Zed, it's..." Bev turned and realized they weren't alone. Besides Vellora and Anders,

Gore and Freddie Silver stood huddled around the clearing. They carried nothing with them, but their nervous faces were illuminated by the strange, glowing orange flowers that seemed about ready to bloom.

"Is that one of my scythes?" Gore asked.

"Erm, yes," Bev said. "I was hoping to bury it."

His eyes widened.

"Trying to stop this magical storm," Bev finished quickly. "Which is wreaking havoc everywhere. We need to figure out who's behind it, and—"

"No one is *behind* the mischief," Andres said with a wave of his hand. "Besides that, we've been waiting for ages to meet. And I think you'll want to hear what I have to say, Bev."

"Will I?" Bev muttered as she stood next to Vellora. "Because I'm not quite sure I want to know what I've stumbled on here."

"You're the one who asked Vellora to reach out to me," Andres said. "Curious about your past. Why do that if you weren't eager to overthrow the queen?"

"Because..." Bev cleared her throat. "I'm sorry...did you say overthrow the queen?"

Andres smiled, but he was the only one to do so. "It's an idea. A spark right now. I've been traveling the country, speaking with like-minded individuals, trying to light the spark of our movement. Things aren't safe for a large portion of people in this country. If you have a hint of magic, you're constantly looking over your shoulder. Wondering when the queen's people are going to take you away. And I say it's time to end that and bring back order."

"Hear, hear," Vellora muttered.

"Does Ida know what you're doing?" Bev said.

"It's *because* of Ida that I'm doing this," Vellora replied. "She puts on a good face, but every time a soldier waltzes into town, she stops sleeping. It's no way to live. There's nothing wrong with who she is, and it's outrageous the queen would want her hunted because of the way she was born."

"I don't disagree, but…" Bev turned to Andres. "So it has been you all this time."

"Me, what?" He blinked. "Attacking Zed? Turning his horses into caterpillars and weapons into bread? Of course not."

"And stealing his potions," Bev reminded him with a click of her tongue. "Well, if it's not you, who is it?"

"I don't know," Andres said. "But I'm grateful for whoever it is, because it's keeping Zed distracted. One or two days of delivering meat with Vellora, and a few episodes without me in town, and I'm off his suspect list. He's too busy chasing down whoever is."

"Meanwhile, someone in town has caused a magical storm," Bev said, gesturing to the sky above them that was still flashing purple. "Zed seemed to think the world was ending."

"Zed's afraid of magic because of what he did to it," Andres said. "But it's a storm. Nothing can be done that can't be undone."

Bev took the gingerbread man out of her pocket and showed it to him. "And what of Zed, eh? Can *this* be undone?"

Andres let out a breath. "Well…Serves him right. Turncoat." But his words didn't seem to have the same passion they'd had before. "Yes, like his horses, we can turn him back."

"With what potions? His were stolen."

"Do you think he's the only one with potion knowledge?" Andres asked. "Who do you think taught him everything he knows?"

Before anyone could answer, there was movement in the bushes behind them. Andres pulled a sharp knife from his belt and held it, while Vellora grabbed a large stick.

"Show yourself," Andres demanded.

Bev feared it would be Casimir and Ollie, but to her shock, Stephen and Feliciano came out, holding knives and looking quite afraid.

"The lot of you, stay where you are," Stephen said, his voice shaking.

"Or better yet," Feliciano said, "step *away* from our flowers."

"Flowers?" Bev spun around, her gaze landing

on the odd orange flowers, which were on the cusp of blooming. As she stared at it, one unfurled completely, glowing brightly.

"*Move!*" Stephen cried, rushing forward.

Bev jumped out of the way as Stephen came at her with his knife bared. But his goal was the flower, or the stalks of pollen that had emerged from the bloom. He carefully ran his knife along the edge of the stalks, and a small collection of black seeds floated down into his hand.

"What are you doing, man?" Andres asked. "And what are these?"

"*Floria Potentia*," Feliciano said, his knife still bared. "A rare and very powerful flower that only blooms on the full moon solstice. And if any one of you harms any of these flowers, we will end you!"

Bev had to laugh, considering the group had already brandished their swords, scythes, and other weapons. But the farmers, seeming to realize the interlopers weren't there to cause them harm, relaxed. Even Vellora put down her stick.

"Who are you?" Bev asked Stephen, who was still harvesting the seeds carefully.

"We're herbologists," Feliciano said with a blush. "We study magical plants."

"Or used to," Stephen said with a sigh. "Before the queen took over."

"I understand completely," Andres said with a laugh as he visibly relaxed. "You said this was a…?"

"*Floria Potentia*," Feliciano said. "It's a rare flower that can be used for many different potions. One of the most powerful plants in existence, in fact."

"So you came here to harvest them?" Bev asked. "I've never seen them growing in the forest before."

"Well, we…had to plant them," Feliciano said, a little evasively.

"And we might've planted…too many," Stephen added, his face turning pink. "And caused the river to overflow."

"So it *was* you two!" Bev glared at them.

"We didn't do it intentionally," Stephen said, holding up his hands. "The flowers naturally release magic as they grow. Since it's a rare flower, only blooming on the solstice full moon, we…erm… planted a lot. Only shot we're going to get for at least another half-century."

"Didn't you know what was going to happen?" Bev asked.

"Neither one of us were alive the last time, of course," Feliciano said. "The writings of the herbologists before us mentioned nothing of having a river overflow, so…"

"We do apologize for causing the magical storm tonight," Stephen said. "But the river should subside, now that the flowers are blooming. Once we harvest the seeds, the flowers stop releasing magic." He deposited the black seeds into a small satchel. "Should make quick work of it."

"Okay, so the flowers were causing the river to overflow," Bev said. "But we still don't know who attacked Zed and his soldiers—"

"It was *meeeeee*!"

Everyone spun around at the low-pitched voice. Out of the dark trees stumbled a small creature with brown skin, a bald head, and pointed ears. His vivid green eyes danced around, unable to stay on one spot as he swayed. And Bev wouldn't have believed he was real, except she knew exactly who he was.

"Officer Nog?"

Chapter Twenty~One

The goblin swaggered around as if he were drunk, and to Bev's surprise, magic shot out of his fingers whenever he pointed. A nearby tree turned into a candy cane, a bush into a large cupcake complete with sprinkles.

"Watch those fingers!" Bev cried, rushing toward the goblin and taking him by the arms to point them down. "What in the world are you doing here, Nog? And why did you attack the soldiers?"

"Why *wouldn't* I?" he declared, his eyes dancing in the dim light. "No-good rotten scoundrels. Forced us all underground. Serves 'em right."

"You know this…thing?" Andres asked, quirking a brow.

"Where did he come from?" Vellora asked.

"It's a long story," Bev said, exasperated. "And he's not normally like this. It must be…must be the magic making him loopy."

"Yes, he's a goblin," Feliciano said, eyeing him. "It's been years since I've seen one, of course. Thought they were all eradicated. They were said to hover around wizards and learn their skills, but never had the amount of magic needed to actually cast."

"Until now, it seems," Stephen said, kneeling to look Nog in the eye. "Fascinating."

"Can someone *do* something to knock him out of it?" Bev snapped, as Nog fought her grip. "Or he's going to turn us all into delicious dinner rolls."

"Oh, I could *gooo* for a dinner *rolll*," he bellowed, his voice echoing into the night sky.

"I need more of my crumble," Bev muttered.

"Erm…your crumble?" Freddie said quietly. "Why do you need that?"

"Because it's laced with iron and willow bark, so it will help him come to his senses," Bev said, struggling as Nog pulled one hand free. "But I don't have any left. It's all gone—"

Freddie blushed as he procured a bowl from a nearby stump.

Bev blinked as she recognized her crumble. "How did you…?"

"I got it for him," Andres said. "It worked so

well on Ida."

"Are you…" Bev surveyed him. No, it wasn't for him. "Hans has magic?"

"Well, he does *now* apparently," Freddie said. "Been spouting sparks from his fingertips for the past week. Andres told me about the river and—"

"Let me *go*, you infernal woman!" Nog bellowed, cutting him off.

"Give me a morsel of it," Bev said, holding out her hand.

Freddie rushed forward and handed her a piece of rhubarb. She managed to pry open the goblin's mouth with his help and deposit the piece inside. Nog sputtered and cursed and broke free as he shook his head. But his eyes, which had been darting around wildly since he'd appeared, suddenly focused on Bev, and that usual look of disdain and disgust appeared.

"What're you doing here?" he snarled then stopped as he looked around. Fear dawned, and he took a nervous step back. "Who are all you people? And for that matter, where am I?"

"You're in the dark forest near Pigsend," Bev said. "Upper Pigsend. You've been…erm…a bit drunk."

"Drunk!" He jumped back, shocked. "Ain't no way."

"The river in Pigsend has been high," Bev said. "Made higher because of someone's *influence*."

Feliciano and Stephen ducked their heads in shame.

"And it's caused all manner of problems in Pigsend," Bev continued. "Clearly, with you, too. How long have you been this way?"

Nog rubbed his head, as if nursing a headache. "Days, I think. I came up to get some food from the market. Then I was gonna stop by that Wormwood house to pick up a phoenix. But…everything got hazy."

"Wormwood?" Vellora gasped. "Bathilda? She has a *phoenix*?"

"It's currently flying over Pigsend," Bev said, suddenly remembering the chaos happening outside the forest with a sinking dread. "Are you in your right mind?"

Nog nodded. "My head is splittin', but—"

"Then we have bigger issues to worry about," Bev said, turning to the rest of those assembled. "We have to get the magic levels down before the whole town is destroyed."

"Destroyed?" Vellora and Freddie shared a look of fear.

"The flowers are blooming," Feliciano said, stepping forward. "So all we need to do is harvest the seeds. As soon as we do, the magic will be severed from the river. That should lower the levels considerably."

"Then we'd better get to harvesting," Bev

snapped. "How many flowers could there be?"

Hundreds, it turned out. The herbologists hadn't had too much care in planting the seeds, and with all the magic in the river, there were bright orange buds everywhere they looked. Feliciano and Stephen quickly instructed the group how to harvest the seeds by scraping them from the stigma, as the herbologists called the long stem in the center of the buds, and the group split up to cover more ground.

As they'd said, once the seeds were removed, the flower withered and died immediately, and the plants surrounding it deflated, too. But as Bev finished harvesting one flower, she'd spot ten more ahead. The effort seemed never-ending.

But as the minutes wore on, the purple tint to the sky grew darker, and the flashes of light diminished. Finally, she saw no more flowers in her general vicinity, and headed back to the clearing, where the rest of the group had assembled, handing over their bags of seeds to the pleased scientists.

"I think that's most of them," Feliciano said with a satisfied smile as he held the bags in his hand. "Can you imagine, Stephen? We've got more seeds than we could've dreamed of!"

"Watch that celebrating," Vellora warned, "until we see what our town looks like."

Bev turned to Nog, who was picking at the rhubarb crumble and trying to avoid scrutiny. "You didn't happen to steal a chest of potions, did you?"

He looked up and grunted. "Maybe I did, maybe I didn't. Either way, I gotta be getting back home. I'm sure I've been missed—"

"Oh, no you don't," Bev said, stepping toward him. "You've got to help us set everything right."

"Do I?" He smirked. "Seems like it was these scientists who caused all the problems with their flowers. I was a helpless victim. Don't gotta—"

"I think you should reconsider that idea, Nog."

Bev couldn't believe her ears. Percival swept in from the dark trees beyond, wearing his robes but not his wizard hat. His eyes were ablaze with fury at Nog as he approached.

"Once again, I find you at the center of mystery revelations, Bev." Percival broke off glaring at Nog to smile at her.

"It's becoming a habit, it seems," Bev said. "But it was quite dangerous for you to come, Percival."

"With all the magic in the air," he said, waving his hand, "I could walk down the street and no one would be the wiser. But," he gestured to Andres, "they will reanimate and have no clue I was here."

"Reani—" Bev's gaze swept the group, and to her surprise, she found them all frozen in place, some mid-conversation.

"This is a fine thing, hiding in the dark forest," Percival said, sounding exasperated as he approached Nog. "The people have needed their food and been waiting on your return."

Nog worked his jaw. "Well, I didn't think I was being appreciated for my good work, so—"

"Oh, bother on that," Bev said. "Nog's been drunk off the magic. He's the one who turned Zed's horses into caterpillars and his weapons into bread. And I'm pretty sure he stole Zed's potions, too."

Percival blinked as he turned back to Nog. "You…did? There must've been some magic up here, then."

"There was," Bev said, pointing to the herbologists who were also frozen. "These two thought it was a good idea to grow *Floria Potentia* in the dark forest. That's what's been causing the excess of magic."

Percival chuckled. "Yes, that'll do it. Especially if you've been able to harvest so many seeds. I daresay this place was up to its eyeballs in magic."

"Hopefully, things go back to normal." She paused, looking down at the gingerbread version of Zed. "Maybe."

"That is a man," Percival said, following her gaze. It wasn't a question. "He was struck by the magical storm?"

Bev nodded. "There's a lot of this going on in Pigsend right now. Giant chickens. That phoenix Nog was sent to retrieve kept bursting into flames. A few houses got turned into flowers." She shook her head. "Can you help?"

Percival shook his head. "It was risky enough for me to leave Lower Pigsend to retrieve this... gentleman. I can't be seen walking through your village. I don't have quite enough magic to stop everyone in their tracks."

Bev's hopes deflated. "But..."

"This might help." Nog cleared his throat and with a small *pop* a chest appeared. Zed's potions. "I think he's got a forgetting potion in here."

"*Now* you're being helpful?" Bev glowered at him as she opened the chest, perusing the vials. "I don't know which ones do what. And I don't know if there's enough to contain everything that's going wrong in Pigsend."

"Not quite," Percival said, brandishing his wand. "If I can steal a few of those seeds, though, I should be able to use them to make more potion—enough to handle whatever chaos you have in Pigsend."

Bev crossed the clearing to pull one of the bags from Feliciano's hand. She could only imagine what the herbologist would say if he could see her using some of his precious seeds. But, she figured he'd caused all the problems, so the least he could do was help solve them.

Percival used his wand to levitate twenty black seeds in the air. They spun for a minute, mixing with some magic from his wand, then with a *pop*, another chest—nearly identical to the one Zed's— appeared. This one was filled with vials, all the same color.

"That should do it," Percival said, putting his wand away. "The river's already subsided greatly, so you shouldn't have anything new come up. But if you do..." He winked. "You know where to find me."

"Thank you," Bev said with a grateful smile before looking to the rest of the group. It was unnerving how they just stood there. "Are you going to unfreeze them?"

"As soon as I'm gone," Percival said. "Well, Nog? Are you coming? Or would you like to continue to wreak havoc on unsuspecting soldiers and nearly get yourself arrested?"

Nog made a noise then rose and followed Percival.

Before the wizard departed, he brandished his wand again, "I hope our next meeting is over something mundane, like tea."

"Likewise," Bev said.

With a *pop,* he was gone, and everyone in the clearing suddenly came back to life.

"Where did he go?" Andres cried.

Vellora spun around. "What happened?"

"I'm missing a bag!" Feliciano gasped.

"Everyone calm down," Bev said, picking up the second chest of potions. "And listen up, because our work's just getting started."

After a quick explanation, Bev, Andres, Vellora, and the farmers took the two chests of potions back into Pigsend. Bev carried gingerbread Zed inside his own chest, but she wasn't quite ready to change him back yet. Not until everything was back to normal.

The river had ebbed, but the chaos was ongoing. The chickens had shrunk to the size of small dogs, but they were still walking around town. Allen and Lillie had retreated to the bakery, and stood in the window, staring wide-eyed at a particularly devilish-looking fowl pecking at the bush in front of the bakery.

Luckily, it was so engrossed in eating the greenery that it didn't notice Bev walking up behind it, uncorking the vial, and sprinkling the potion on it. With a *zip*, the chicken shrank to a normal size, and Bev quickly scooped it up into her arms.

Lillie and Allen ran outside, shocked. "Where'd you get that?"

"Long story," Bev said, thumbing at the chest at her feet. "But we've got plenty of it."

Allen took the small chicken, and Lillie joined the group rounding up the rest of them. Bev had thought they would run out of potion, but every time she opened the chest, more magically appeared.

"You need to bake something lovely for Percival," Bev muttered to Lillie.

"Perci—" She gasped. "He was here?"

Bev told her what had happened in the forest

and she made a face. "That little sneak, Nog. Drunk on magic, sure. Drunk on ale, too, I'd wager."

As the group worked their way through town, saving the townsfolk trapped in their houses, those townsfolk followed. And as before, every time Bev handed out a vial of forgetting potion, another would take its place. Soon they'd rounded up all Rosie's chickens and placed them back in her yard, much to her delight.

"Thank you!" she cried from her window.

Next was the Brewer house, which was still a flower hanging off a vine that reached into the sky. Bev wasn't sure how much potion would be needed to tackle *that,* but it turned out to be two vials—one to shrink the vine, one to transform the flower back into a house.

"Oh, Bev!" Shasta squealed as their house settled right back where it had been. "Once again, you're a lifesaver!"

"Has anyone seen Bathilda?" Bev called. "Or her phoenix?"

On cue, a sad-looking bird stumbled out of Etheldra's tea shop. He coughed out a puff of smoke, then fell over asleep.

"What happened to him?" Bev said.

"Doused him with a bit of iron water," Etheldra said, walking out of her shop looking pleased. "He thought he was going to set my shop on fire, but he had another think coming, eh?"

"We've already had enough fires in town this year," Earl replied.

Bev smiled, grateful. She gazed around town, and while there were more large chicken clawmarks than usual, and a few roofs that would need to be repaired, there didn't seem to be anything else amiss.

"What a night, eh?" Etheldra said. "Where's that Zed when you need him? Thought he was supposed to put a stop to all this."

"He's erm…indisposed at the moment," Bev said. "Which…I should probably tend to him and his soldiers…"

"Do you have to?" Andres asked, walking up with Vellora and Ida in tow. "He's much nicer as a gingerbread man."

"Yes," Bev said with a look. "And I've got to find his soldiers, too. Jemma was turned into a tree, but I haven't seen Ollie or Casimir—"

"Those scaredy cats?" Ida barked a laugh. "They've been hiding in your root cellar. Saw them scamper in during the storm."

"Well, then," Bev said. "Let's get back to the inn."

~

Ollie and Casimir were, in fact, hiding in Bev's root cellar, carrying the iron material Bev had sent them to bury out in the fields. She was more than a little miffed they'd hidden instead of helped, but at least she didn't have to dig the iron objects back up.

She poured the vial of potion onto the beautiful golden-leafed tree in the backyard, and with a *pop* it turned back into Jemma. She swayed, wide-eyed, before her fellow soldiers grasped her arms and helped walk her back to the inn, with Bev in tow. She placed the chest on the table and opened it. Only one vial remained. And when she pulled it and the gingerbread version of Zed out, the chest disappeared into nothing.

"What in the—" Casimir said.

"I wouldn't question anything right now," Andres said with a warning tone. "Considering she's about to turn your boss human again."

He wisely closed his mouth.

Bev uncorked the vial and poured it onto the gingerbread man. It stretched and squished before letting out a *pop*. In a flash, Zed was lying on the table, spreadeagled and blinking at the ceiling in confusion. He sat up quickly, grabbing his head, before looking around at those gathered.

"What in the world happened?" Zed asked. "Is the storm over? Why do I taste ginger? Is—"

"Everything's back to normal," Bev said, glancing at the clock. "Happy solstice."

Chapter Twenty~Two

Bev was happy when the sun rose the next morning, and Pigsend was tranquil. Everything *did* seem to have gone back to normal. She didn't know how much Zed could've heard in his baked form, but if he had questions, he didn't ask them. On the other hand, it gave Allen great pleasure to hear what he'd been transformed into.

Feliciano and Stephen hadn't come back to the inn, which suited Bev fine. The next time she saw those flower seeds would be too soon, as helpful as they'd ended up being. It was a good thing the solstice and full moon were once every fifty years or so. She hoped the herbologists would make a rather *detailed* note about what happened when one planted too many flowers, for future generations.

At seven, Lillie brought over muffins and wished Bev a happy solstice as she placed them on the counter. "Wild night, eh?" She leaned across the counter. "Still can't believe it was *Nog*. What was he even doing up here?"

"I think he and Percival had a falling out of sorts. Either way, he went back." She pointed down. "But I'm grateful, at least, he had the chest of potions. Don't know what we would've done otherwise."

A door opened upstairs, and Kemp made his way down the hall, his face a mask of worry and fear.

"Oh, Kemp, I wasn't sure if you were still here," Bev said with a laugh. "Did you make it through last night all right?"

"Dreadful city you have here," Kemp said, walking up with his bag in hand. "Can't imagine anyone would want to live here. I'm happy to be on my way as fast as I can. Did you *see* those chickens last night?"

"I did," Bev said. "Well, I can't say that sort of thing is normal for Pigsend, but—"

"I would like to speak to the bakers before I leave," Kemp said. "Is that possible?"

"Oh, um. Hi." Lillie waved at him. "What can I do for you?"

He marched forward, and for a brief moment,

Bev thought he was going to arrest her. Instead, he held out his hand. "My name is Kemp Abora. I'm from the town of Silverkeep."

"Very nice to meet you," Lillie said with an uncertain chuckle.

"Sorry." He cleared his throat. "I'm here on behalf of the mayor. You see, before the war, we had a large population of mag...erm...creatures Her Majesty deemed unfit." He adjusted his cloak, and Bev wasn't sure whether he supported that or not. "So after the war, we found ourselves without many industries that keep a town afloat. Blacksmiths, cobblers, tailors, that sort of thing. The mayor sent me on a mission to find interested parties to move to Silverkeep and restart those businesses."

"O-oh!" Lillie blinked wildly. "Well, I don't think..."

"With a town this size, surely two bakers is too many," he continued, glancing between Lillie and Bev. "The bakery is so small. I'm sure you're tripping over each other."

"Lillie?" Bev turned to her. "Is this something you might want to do?"

Lillie licked her lips and looked around. "If it's all the same, I..." She cleared her throat. "You know, I do really like it here. And I've signed a contract with Wilda to rent her room through the year, so..." She smiled apologetically at Kemp. "Not right now. But if the opportunity is still there in the future, I'd love to consider it."

He nodded, a little disappointed. "We'd love to have you. You've got quite the artistry, the likes of which we haven't seen since..." He sighed. "If it's a 'not right now' then I must be on my way. Need to chat with that blacksmith's apprentice to see if she's ready to strike out on her own."

"That's a great idea," Bev said. "Gilda's been nearing the end of her training for a while now. I'm sure she'd love to hear you out."

At that, he brightened and donned his cap. "Glad this dreadful week wasn't a complete waste of time." He chuckled and picked up his bag. "Off to speak with Ms. Gilda."

And with that, he was out the door.

"That is incredible," Lillie said with a laugh. "All this time, he was here looking for people to move to his town? What a curious fellow."

"You should consider it," Bev said. "Not that I'm in any hurry for you to leave, but it might be good to spread your wings."

"Maybe someday," Lillie said with a sigh. "But for now, I've got to get these solstice pies in the oven before Etheldra murders us!"

~

Around eight, Andres appeared on the upstairs landing, and a moment later, so did Zed. They eyed each other before Zed held out his hand to let Andres go first. Andres hesitated, perhaps unsure if

Zed was going to stab him in the back, but walked down the stairs.

"Happy solstice," Andres said. "What a beautiful day it is out there."

"Glad for it," Bev said. "And glad everyone is safe. Zed, are you feeling all right?"

He nodded, picking up a muffin and examining it. "I feel I should discuss certain things that happened last night—"

"Oh, come off it, man," Andres said. "Bev could've put you next door in the bakery to be eaten by a child, but instead she made sure you were safe and sound. You—"

"*But* in light of your service to me and my soldiers, not to mention the rest of the town, I'm going to let it slide," Zed finished before glaring at Andres and taking a big bite of the muffin.

"I daresay I wouldn't have answers to give you," Bev said. "I'm as confused as you are. Just happy the storm seemed to pass. I suppose it got it all out of its system, yeah? Like a bad rainstorm?"

Zed chewed thoughtfully. "That is certainly one explanation."

"In any case, I hear we have an outstanding fireworks display to look forward to tonight," Bev said. "And I've got lots of laundry to tend to, so if you'll excuse me..."

Bev busied herself with cleaning Feliciano and Stephen's room, then Kemp's, hoping that, since she didn't hear cross words or weapons being drawn downstairs, Andres and Zed were remaining civil. When she knocked on Solan's door, she was surprised when it opened.

"Happy solstice," Solan said with a bright smile. "It's a beautiful day, isn't it? About time for me to be moving on."

"Is…erm…everything fine out in the dark forest? I didn't see you again last night."

"I saw a gaggle arriving and thought it was time to make my escape," they said with a laugh. "They certainly seemed an intense bunch. I didn't want to be in the middle of whatever they were discussing."

Intense was correct. "And you're okay to travel?"

"Yes." They inhaled deeply. "It seems whatever was bothering the river has left. It's still high, of course, but a normal amount. Staying within its banks, so to speak."

"Well, we do appreciate your assistance," Bev said. "Where are you headed to next?"

"I haven't a clue," they said with a sigh. "Wherever the wind takes me, I suppose."

~

Bev spent the day doing her usual chores, and couldn't be happier about it. The inn was hot, but washing the sheets outside was quite refreshing. Even Biscuit laid about on the grass, his tail slapping on the ground every so often as he slept. Bev reset all the rooms, finding as she brought the clean sheets up to Solan's room there was just a mild scent of basil hanging in the air. She supposed it wasn't the worst scent to have around. Might keep the spiders from taking up residence, too.

Once her chores were done, she took another turn around town, searching for where she could offer help in the cleanup. Etheldra and Earl were getting her shop back to normal, as the phoenix seemed to have taken up residence in there after it exploded. Besides a couple of singed chairs, nothing else seemed ruined.

"Ready for the fireworks show this evening?" Earl announced as Bev walked in.

"Ready for the solstice to be over," Bev replied.

Earl frowned, and Etheldra tutted at him. "Earl's been looking forward to this all year long. We can't let a little magical storm ruin his fun."

"Suppose not," Bev said. "Looking forward to it. Has Shasta been in yet?"

"Gave her the day off, what with her house getting turned into a flower and all," Etheldra said. "But I told her to be here bright and early tomorrow."

Earl cleared his throat and tapped his finger to his nose.

"I mean," Etheldra said with a bit of difficulty, "I asked if she wouldn't mind opening the shop for me, so I could have a bit of rest. She gladly agreed."

~

Bev continued her tour around town, finding Rosie out amongst her chickens, feeding them corn from a basket. She smiled brightly as Bev approached and walked up to the fence.

"I can't thank you enough, Bev," Rosie said. "I'm not quite sure what happened last night."

"Just a fluke," Bev said, nodding at the chickens. "Everyone safe and accounted for?"

"Oh, every last one." She stared at them lovingly. "And they seem back to their usual lovely selves, too."

Bev wasn't too sure about that, as they flapped their wings at the fence angrily. "Well, if you need anything else, let me know. Glad you're all right."

"Another loaf of that bread would be lovely," Rosie said, a little lightly. "For my nerves, you know. Just the thing."

Bev smiled. "Absolutely."

Typically, she didn't have anyone new at the inn on the summer solstice itself, as everyone was usually where they wanted to be. But she still wanted to assemble a smaller dinner, as Zed and his soldiers, as well as Andres, would be there. However, when she walked into the butcher shop to place her order, she was told dinner would be taken care of.

"Roasting a pig," Vellora announced proudly. "I assume everyone's going to be at the fireworks tonight, too. So you can take the night off, Bev."

Between the roasting pig, the solstice pies that

came out of the bakery, and the fruits and vegetables the farmers brought in from out of town, the town square became an impromptu festival for all the local folks. Earl grabbed chairs from the town hall, and Ida helped Vellora roll tables out from the tea shop and move benches from the schoolhouse. The sun set slowly in the distance, and farmers Dane Sterling and Eldred Nest and the miller Sonny Gray struck up a lively tune on their instruments. It was about as festive as the wedding the month before, but without the curses and chaos.

After the sun finally dipped beneath the horizon, Earl announced it was time for the fireworks show. Those gathered brought out blankets and settled on the dirt around town, gazes up at the stars. Earl set off the first one, and it exploded in beautiful colors against the clear sky. Bev was reminded of the magical storm, and the fearsome power the night before.

Her gaze landed on Zed, and she couldn't help but sympathize with his way of thinking. The magical folk *had* been out of control the night before. With giant chickens and phoenixes bursting into flames, not to mention the way everyone had been feeling so poorly for so long, it was easy to believe life was easier without magical creatures in it.

And yet…her gaze shifted to Lillie, who was chatting animatedly with Ida, Vellora, and Freddie and Hans Silver—who seemed completely cured.

Hans looked to be all better, perhaps due to the last of Bev's crumble his husband had brought to him from the inn, or perhaps because the river was gone. Bev didn't even know what kind of magic he possessed, but it was enough to encourage his husband to meet with Andres.

Speaking of whom… Vellora's commander was walking up to Bev. He stood next to her, his face illuminated by the exploding fireworks, and was quiet for a long time.

"It's beautiful, isn't it?" Bev said.

"Mm." He turned to her. "I confess, the solstice does make me sad, because the days will get darker and darker until the winter solstice."

"I don't mind the dark. It comes with cooler temperatures," Bev said with a laugh. "Are you on your way as well? Headed back…home?"

He eyed her, but Bev realized he wasn't actually looking at her. Rather, his gaze was on the crowd beyond, including Zed and his soldiers, who were out of earshot.

"What you stumbled upon last night—" Andres began.

"Is not something I need to know about," Bev said. "Whatever machinations you're planning, I don't want to be involved. I'm a simple innkeeper —"

"Are you?"

She turned to him with a frown. "You told me

you had nothing to share about my past,"

He glanced at Zed. "The truth has a habit of coming out, no matter how deep it's been buried. And you're right: you're better suited knowing what's coming than to be blindsided."

Bev held her breath.

"I have nothing more to share than what I already told you," Andres said. "The magical amulet, the laelaps, all of it points to you being a powerful wizard in a past life."

Bev nodded, feeling a bit faint. "What happened to me?"

"I'm honestly not sure. It would take an incredible amount of magic to make a wizard forget who they were—and forget they had magic, too. Something more than a simple forgetting potion."

"Do you think I did it to myself?" Bev asked. "Or was it…done to me?"

"That's the bigger question," he said. "It's possible your past self wanted to hide your abilities in a new world without magic and decided to take the plunge. But that would leave you vulnerable and, as I said, the past has a way of catching up with you. So it seems to me that someone did this to you. Perhaps to keep you from your magic. Perhaps…" He nodded toward Zed, whose back was to him. "To nullify an adversary that was too powerful to contain otherwise."

"Do you think Zed knows?" Bev asked.

"If he does, you'll never get it out of him, no matter how many times you turn him back from a gingerbread man," Andres said.

"Where do I go from here?" Bev asked.

"There are things in motion that cannot be stopped," Andres said. "People like Freddie and Vellora, eager to protect their loved ones from overzealous soldiers, are growing tired of always looking over their shoulders. The magical folk are still around—somewhere—and they'll tire of hiding eventually."

Bev didn't like the sound of that. "But war? Haven't we all been through enough?"

He lifted a shoulder. "Perhaps. But perhaps the worst is yet to come. I, for one, am going to fight until every creature in this land is free to live as they please." He smiled at her. "The question is, Bev, are you going to do the same?"

Bev continues her adventures in

Acknowlegments

As always, first thanks goes to my husband for believing in me and for managing the toddler in the evenings. Thanks, also, go to my son, for continuing to insist upon his six o'clock bedtime so I could write yet another book in the dark. Shout-out to Ms. Rachel, too. You're the real MVP.

Thanks to Chelsea, Danielle, and Lisa for being the all-star team who helps keep me going. And to my writer pals, Brett, Kelsey, and Emily, for keeping me sane.

Also By the Author

The Princess Vigilante Series

Brynna has been protecting her kingdom as a masked vigilante until one night, she's captured by the king's guards. Instead of arresting her, the captain tells her that her father and brother have been assassinated and she must hang up her mask and become queen.

The Princess Vigilante series is a four-book young adult epic fantasy series, perfect for fans of Throne of Glass and Graceling.

The Seod Croi Chronicles

After her father's murder, princess Ayla is set to take the throne — but to succeed, she needs the magical stone her evil stepmother stole. Fortunately, wizard apprentice Cade and knight Ward are both eager to win Ayla's favor.

A Quest of Blood and Stone is the first book in the *Seod Croi* chronicles and is available now in eBook, paperback, and hardcover.

About the Author

S. Usher Evans was born and raised in Pensacola, Florida. After a decade of fighting bureaucratic battles as an IT consultant in Washington, DC, she suffered a massive quarter-life-crisis. She found fighting dragons was more fun than writing policy, so she moved back to Pensacola to write books full-time. She currently resides there with her husband and kids, and frequently can be found plotting on the beach.

Visit S. Usher Evans online at:
http://www.susherevans.com/